LAS CUCARACHAS

A NOVEL BY
YONGSOO PARK

AKASHIC BOOKS
New York

Published by Akashic Books
©2004 Yongsoo Park
Layout by Sohrab Habibion

ISBN: 1-888451-56-4
Library of Congress Control Number: 2003116593
All rights reserved
First printing
Printed in Canada

Akashic Books
PO Box 1456
New York, NY 10009
Akashic7@aol.com
www.akashicbooks.com

For So Jene

CHAPTER 1

A CHEWED-UP NERF flies out of nowhere and smacks me in the head when me and Steven are about ten yards past the super. I turn around to see who threw it and there's Fatty, smiling like some retard. It's not even 9 and the bastard's already got a thick red ring around his mouth from all the ramen he eats. The jerkoff must go through a box every three days.

"Yo, my mom told me everything," he blurts out. "They broke into your apartment, right? It's 'cuz they think Korean people keep bags of cash in the house."

I stare at his beady little eyes, wondering just how any kid could be so damn stupid. I mean, yeah our apartment got robbed and my Atari and all 42 games are gone, but why the hell's he gotta remind me for? The kid's just so damn stupid sometimes. I mean, everyone's always going on and on about how Korean kids are super smart and born doing the times table, but what the hell happened to Fatty?

Take the kid's name for instance. I guess Taek-Won ain't as bad as some super retarded f.o.b. names like Man Yoo Suck or Oh Yoo Bum, but it still sounds like the beginning of "tae kwon do" or part of some corny rap like, "Microphone check, take one, take two, yo, let's go." Either way, the name's pretty damn corny. So I don't blame the kid for chucking it. I just don't think Fatty's much better. But he doesn't seem to mind. He seems almost to like it.

Anyway, enough about the dumb fuck's stupid name. I don't appreciate getting whacked in the head, especially first thing in the morning. So I pick the ball up off the ground and fling it hard at his round bowling-ball head. For a kid who hardly weighs nothing, I got me a pretty good arm, so the ball's a bullet. Not that I ever got it measured with radar or anything, but it's fast, at least 95 miles per hour, if not 125. If the Mets ever got their act together, they woulda signed me up already. With me and Jesse Orosco, who's also a lefty, we'd be invincible. Sure, we'd be even better with Tom Seaver, but the bozos who run the team traded him to the White Sox, so what the hell can you do?

The only thing is, Fatty ducks out the way like the chicken-shit he is, so the ball hits the side of the super's bananamobile instead. There's no dent or scratch—how could there be when the ball's just a big fat sponge?—but the super just has to make a big deal out of it anyway 'cuz he ain't got nothing better to do than pick his nose and scratch his ass when he's not mopping the hall-way. So he crawls out from under the hood real slow and stares at me like he's got static. Not that I care. He can stare all day if he wants. I ain't scared of the son of a bitch, so the fuck with him. If he starts with me, I'll call immigration on his ass.

What's the big fucking deal anyway? It ain't like we keyed his car or snapped off the fucking antenna, which we oughtta do 'cuz the jerkoff deserves it, or like the asshole's car's even worth any-thing. I know for a fact that the dickweed got it off some welfare auction out in Pennsylvania for 25 bucks, which, if you ask me, was a major rip-off. But that's what you get for being Puerto Rican and having a birdbrain.

Still, I got manners and I don't wanna start nothing, so I say, "Sorry, super. It was an accident."

The super takes a puff off his 25-cent cigar and says, "Forget it, boys. No harm, no foul. I was a kid once, too, you know. Here's your ball back. Now run along and enjoy your summer."

Yeah, right.

Maybe shit like that happens on *Fantasy Island*. But if Tattoo were on our block, we'd just kick his and Mr. Roarke's ass like we do Hindu Tim's.

In real life, the super waddles over to where the ball is, on account of how his one leg is shorter than the other, picks it up, then points to the sign on the wall with his cigar. I've lived in the Holland all my life. I know what the sign says: *"NO LOITERING, NO LOUD MUSIC, NO BALL PLAYING."* And I know what it means: *"The super's a dick."*

So the douchebag says, "How many times I gotta tell you fucking kids not to play in front of the building!"

"We weren't playing. It was an accident," I say.

But the jackass couldn't care less and I might as well be speaking Chinese, which I don't, by the way, 'cuz I hate chinks more than I do spics, even those who take Nerfs off kids and toss 'em in the trunks of their crappy bananamobiles.

I oughtta kick the scumbag's ass and make the motherfucker cry like a little baby, but it's Fatty's ball, and he ain't doing shit to get it back, so I sure as hell ain't gonna do shit, neither.

So I just turn around and start walking up the block, keeping my eyes on the ground the whole time 'cuz of all the dog shit everywhere.

Of course, now that the super's not in our faces no more, good old Fatty, who just stood there the whole time like some scared little kid about to pee his pants, starts running his mouth like crazy about how he's gonna kick the super's ass. If I had a dime for every time Fatty said that bullshit I'd be a goddamn millionaire by now.

Halfway up the block, Fatty turns to me and says, "Why'd you throw the ball like that for, bro? You knew the super was right there."

Talk about gratitude. The son of a bitch actually makes it sound like the whole thing was my fault. So I say, "You knew he was there, too, Fatty. Why'd you throw the ball at me?"

"You owe me a ball, bro."

"Fine, Fatty. I'll get you a damn ball! Just stop fucking whining."

"Yeah, right. With what money?"

Fucking Fatty's always gotta get in the last word.

A couple of steps later, he says, "So did you call 5-0 or what?"

There he is again, yapping away about my apartment getting robbed. You figure the kid would take a hint from the first time and shut the fuck up already, but he's got fucking rocks for brains. So instead of an answer, I whack a Mountain Dew can with my foot and send it flying under a parked car out to the middle of the street. It's a good kick. If we were playing kick-the-can, it'd get everyone out of jail and make life hell for whoever's "it."

"Well, what happened, bro? Did you call 5-0 or what?"

"Yeah, we called 'em," I finally say, 'cuz I know there's no shutting the bastard up.

"So what did they do?"

"Nothing."

"Nothing?" Fatty makes his I'm-stupid-and-confused face, which is exactly the same as his I'm-hungry face. "I don't get it. What d'you mean, nothing?"

"What d'you think I mean, Fatty? Nothing."

"Didn't they at least dust for fingerprints or take photos like they do in the movies?"

"No, Fatty. They didn't do shit."

"What about all the stuff you lost?"

"What about it?"

"Are they gonna try to get it back or what?"

"They ain't gonna do shit."

"What d'you mean? They gotta do something, don't they?"

"Goddamn, Fatty. What the hell's your problem? I told you already. They ain't gonna do shit, all right. So stop bugging me about it."

I guess he finally gets it 'cuz he starts shaking his head real slow, then says, "That's messed up, bro. You got dissed. You got dissed by 5-0."

As much as I hate to admit it, the bastard's right. Not that I ever had much faith in cops. I know all they ever do is eat donuts and go around hassling people for no reason just 'cuz they got badges and guns and think they're so fucking tough. I don't know why cops are such fucking assholes. But the way I see it, you gotta be one ugly, useless dickhead of a kid to wanna grow up and be one.

Of course, even knowing all that, a part of me still expected them to do more than just write up some crummy police report and tell us to get better locks in case of next time. They might as well tell us to go fuck ourselves.

"Yo, we should go talk to Africa and Jin, bro. They were out here all day yesterday. Maybe they saw who stole your shit," says Fatty.

I just nod. Maybe they did and maybe they didn't. All I know is, I ain't gonna get my hopes up. I know better. Shit like that might happen in the movies, but I know it don't happen in real life. So I ain't about to drop everything and start looking for my shit like some dumb kid in some stupid detective story snooping around dark alleys and knocking on locked doors. Fuck Encyclopedia Brown and his corny ass.

Anyway, when we get to the corner, these two black guys from the car wash are standing there, holding their stomachs and cracking up like they just seen the funniest shit. The bigger guy, who's got on Gazelles and is all cut up like he just came out of jail, sees us and points up at the sky.

We look up and see a pair of blue Pumas hanging off the power line. I don't know why they think this is so damn funny. There's gotta be at least a hundred pairs of sneakers hanging off power lines all over the place. So some kid threw them up there, big fucking deal.

But Fatty gets all serious anyway and says, in this way like he's so damn proud of himself, "Yo, I'll bet you a hundred dollars someone took those Pumas off some kid and threw them up there."

"No shit, Sherlock. You figure that out all by yourself?"

Any kid except Fatty would know I was being sarcastic, but Fatty just grins and says, "You know I'm right, bro. You owe me a hundred bucks. I'll take cash money. Only 10s and 20s."

I give him the middle finger instead and tell him to keep the change.

Then, just as we're about to cut out of there, the same car wash guy points at me and says, "Nice shirt, son!"

Fatty looks over at the guy, then at my shirt, which has a picture of some black guy with hair like Medusa's and the dates *"1945–1981."*

"You even know who that is on your shirt, son?" says the car wash guy with this look on his face like he thinks it's so fucking amusing that a little Chinese kid could have a shirt with a black guy on it.

So I look the guy right in his Gazelles and shout, "How the fuck do I know, motherfucker? Mind your own damn business and keep washing cars!"

Yeah, right!

Of course, Fatty starts snickering like crazy 'cuz he knows my shirt's some crappy hand-me-down that my mom got from her work. It's bad enough I gotta wear garbage like that all the time. I don't need fucking Fatty laughing at me.

So I turn to the fat fuck and say, "What's so funny?"

"Nothing," he says, playing it off like he wasn't just laughing at me a second ago.

I shove him hard in the chest anyway, and he stumbles back a couple of steps right into a pile of green-brown dog shit that's so fresh it's actually steaming.

"Fuck!" he says. "Why the hell'd you push me for, bro?"

"You know why."

He gives me this look like he'd shoot me if he still had his BB gun. Not that I'm worried. Maybe some other kid might do something like that or even just take a swing at me, but Fatty's super soft no matter how much shit he talks about kicking people's asses. So I know I ain't got a thing to worry about.

"You're fucked up, bro. I just got these, too," he says, then starts scraping his shelltops back and forth against the pavement like that's somehow gonna get the shit out from in between the treads.

All of a sudden, Steven, who's been following us the whole time but who's so damn quiet you forget he's even around, starts laughing out loud and blurts out, in his super girlish voice, "You're retarded, Fatty!"

It's the first thing the kid's said the whole morning. And knowing him, it'll probably be the only thing he says the whole day. I don't know why the kid's all weird like that, but he just is.

Anyway, Fatty's face turns bright red in half a second. As much crap as he takes from me, there's no way in hell he's gonna let some puny little kid like Steven talk shit to him, at least not right to his face.

So he gets right up in the kid's face and shouts, "Shut the hell up, you little freak!"

That's about all it takes for Steven's face to drop and for him to get all teary-eyed. I don't know who to feel bad for. Fatty shouldn't yell at the kid, but the kid shouldn't get all sad and wussy just 'cuz some fat bastard yelled at him. I mean, how the hell's he ever gonna get through life if he gets like that every time some fatass yells at him?

All I know is it don't matter who's right or wrong. I gotta look out for the kid 'cuz he's my brother, whether I like it or not. So I turn to Fatty and say, "Leave the kid alone! He ain't done nothing to you!"

Fatty looks right at me and says, "You're messed up, bro. You and your brother."

"It's your own damn fault."

"Yeah, yeah," he says, then lifts his foot to check the bottom of his sneakers. Not that it makes a difference. He can scrape all morning and check a thousand times. He's still gonna be trailing shit-smell all day.

I guess the big black guy knows that, too, 'cuz he says, "Don't waste your time, kid. You ain't never gonna get that shit off."

Fatty looks up and just stares at the guy. Then he opens his big mouth and says, "Fuck you, motherfucker."

This time it's no joke, and the guy stares at Fatty like he can't believe his ears. Neither can I. I mean, Fatty can be pretty damn stupid sometimes, but this is beyond stupid.

This huge vein on the side of the guy's neck starts throbbing. Then the guy takes a step toward Fatty and says, "What the hell'd you say, you little punk?"

CHAPTER 2

I OUGHTTA JUST mind my own damn business and let Fatty get his ass kicked for being so fucking stupid, but we're all part of the Warriors, so I gotta watch his back no matter how retarded he is. Before you get all excited about how we ain't nothing but a bunch of biters, I know the name's corny and I know it's from that movie. So sue me. I never said we were original. By the way, we didn't invent kick-the-can or breakdancing, neither.

The Warriors are me, Fatty, Africa, and Jin. Roman used to be a member, too, but he sort of quit 'cuz he hates my guts. Not that I blame the guy. I mean, yeah, I messed up. And I guess I shouldn't have done what I did to the guy. But I ain't gonna be all on the guy's dick just 'cuz of that. The way I see it, he should be man enough to drop it. If he's gonna be a baby and hold grudges, the hell with him. The Warriors are better off without him.

We ain't exactly a gang, at least not like KP or the Goblins. We're more like a crew, which means all of us have grown up together, so we look out for each other, sort of like how Hanibal looks after Face, B.A., and Murdoch.

Take school for instance. Now, I ain't gonna tell you that I.S. 233 is the craziest, toughest, scariest school around, where kids get jumped every time they go out in the hallway or step into the bathroom. But it definitely ain't no place for wusses, which is why it means something that even the crazy black kids from the projects, who mess with *everybody*, leave us alone. It's 'cuz they know messing with us is suicide, hara-kiri, and Death Wish I and II.

We once fought sixty black kids in the train station and won. Left half those cocksuckers with broken ribs and bloody noses, screaming in pain and crying for their mamas.

Like hell we did!

Fatty couldn't fight himself out of a paper bag even though he talks a lot of shit and goes to Tiger Chung Lee's Tae Kwon Do

12

School. As for Africa and Jin, well, you haven't met them yet, but take my word for it, they ain't much tougher than Fatty. Now, does that mean that I can fight like crazy and can beat up kids twice my size?

Not really. I can fight okay, mostly 'cuz I've been in a lot of fights and ain't afraid to take a punch, which is why everyone's always saying how I got a lot of guts. I don't know if that's true, but that's the thing about guts. Even if all you ever do is get beat up a lot and never land a punch, someone will always tell you how you got a lot of guts.

Anyway, the real reason even the black kids from the projects leave us alone is 'cuz of Jin's older brother B.J., who's all guts and the toughest, baddest motherfucker ever to come out of the Holland. It's 'cuz of him that Mom's always telling me not to hang out with Jin so much, which just shows you how different kids and grown-ups think.

Not that Mom has any real reason to worry 'cuz B.J. went to Korea about a year ago to go to the army and look after his sick grandmother, which was a good thing 'cuz the Goblins were getting him into a lot of deep shit.

But this one time, before he left, he showed up at our school and fought ten big black kids, all dickless wannabe big-mouths who claimed to be down with Zulu Nation, 'cuz they stole Jin's train pass.

I don't know where B.J. learned to fight, but I've never seen no one take down as many guys as quickly as he did. It was almost like some Bruce Lee movie except he didn't make no weird noises and the guys going down and eating dirt weren't all corny Chinese guys in karate outfits.

Anyway, you should have seen how those kids were the next day. Me and Jin would go right up to them and curse them out to their faces and say shit about their mothers and their sisters and their grandmothers, and not one of 'em would do shit back.

Of course, none of that does us no good now 'cuz B.J.'s a thousand miles away and the only thing the car wash guy gives a shit about is that some little fat Chinese kid just cursed him out to his face.

So the guy grabs Fatty by the throat and is about to snap his neck in half, when I finally wise up and think to say, "It's all my fault."

The guy turns to me and says, "What?"

"It's all my fault. I shouldn't have done it."

"Done what?"

"My mom made me promise that I wouldn't mess with him, but I couldn't help it. It's all my fault."

"What the hell are you talking about, kid?"

"My cousin just came here from Korea. I'm supposed to be teaching him English, but I've been teaching him all the wrong words. He doesn't even know they're curses. He thinks 'fuck you, motherfucker' means 'have a nice day.'"

The guy looks at me, then at Fatty, like he's not sure what to make of what I just said. I'd do the same thing if I was him 'cuz there are so many bullshit artists out there.

But I gotta make the guy believe me, so I turn to Fatty and tell him real quick in Korean what to do next. That's the good thing about being able to speak another language—it can get you out of some tight spots.

Fatty smiles, then does exactly what I say. He starts bowing like crazy, then says, "Fuck you, motherfucker. Faggotass. Suck my dick. Son of a bitch," in this way that sounds almost like he's singing some corny song.

"See. He doesn't even know what he's saying. He thinks he's saying good words. So it's not his fault. I shouldn't have tricked him. I'm sorry."

"Fuck you, motherfucker. Faggotass. Suck my dick. Son of a bitch," Fatty says again, bowing and smiling.

"Does he know how to say anything else in English?" asks the guy.

"No. Just curses."

"Goddamn." The guy shakes his head, then looks right at me like he's pissed, but not really, the way people do when they're not sure to be mad at you or not. "Tell him those are curses. And teach him some good words, all right?"

"Sure."

"Now go on. Get outta here."

We start walking away, and I have to bite down hard on my lip to keep from losing it. It's like the time we suckered Hindu Tim to be it in manhunt, then went home to eat dinner while he kept looking for us up and down the block for another two hours. Goddamn! How stupid can you get? Fuck you, motherfucker. Faggotass. Suck my dick. Son of a bitch.

CHAPTER 3

I T'S SO FUCKING hot out, there's no one in the handball court except for this crazy old white guy who's always there whacking the shit out of his paddleball and sucking on his cigar like he needs it to breathe. That's the thing with all the old white guys in our neighborhood. They're always doing the weirdest fucking things.

We go on to the stickball lot, where Africa's busy selling jumping jacks to a bunch of little kids who look too soft even for sparklers. Knowing little kids, one of 'em will probably end up on the news with a hand blown off, and everyone on TV will go on and on about how fireworks are evil and ruining young people's lives. They have a point, but then again, you gotta be one stupid fucking moron to lose a finger lighting bottle rockets.

Not that I know why Africa even bothers. What he should do is take the train to Chinatown and get himself grosses for ten bucks. Instead, he gets the jumping jacks for twenty cents a pack off this guy named Baby at the arcade and sells them for a quarter, which basically means he does all that running around for a lousy nickel.

Anyway, as soon as we go over to Africa, Fatty tells him, "You got money?"

Africa nods.

"How much?"

Africa doesn't say nothing. Instead, he turns to me and says, "Diego's been talking shit about you all morning, Pete."

"Yeah? What's he been saying?"

"I don't know what's up with him. But he's been going around telling everybody how no one in the park can strike him out, including you 'cuz you throw like a girl."

Coming from anyone else, that would sound like instigating, like he was trying to sucker me into fighting Diego for no reason.

But I know Africa ain't like that. He's the only kid I know who really doesn't like watching other kids fight.

"You want me to kick that punk's ass for you, Pete?" says Fatty. "'Cuz I'll do it, bro. I'll take that sucker out."

I don't say nothing 'cuz the whole thing's too ridiculous. Diego can say whatever he wants, but there's no way in hell he can even touch my stuff 'cuz the kid couldn't hit a fucking beach ball.

Anyway, while I'm just standing there, Fatty starts talking Africa's ear off about our run-in with the car wash guy. Of course, the way he tells it, the guy was scared out of his mind and Fatty was just about to kick his ass when I ruined it all by breaking it up.

If it were some other day, I might just let the kid run his mouth like that and tell one big fat lie after another, but I ain't in the mood for Fatty's bullshit. So I say, "Stop lying, Fatty. You know you would've got your ass kicked."

"Hell no, bro. I've beat up guys way bigger than that. Fighting big guys ain't nothing. All you gotta do is kick them in the balls."

"You're just lucky the guy fell for it. Next time you do something that stupid, you're on your own."

Fatty plays if off like he didn't hear me and sweeps some broken glass toward the fence with his foot. Some bum must have gone nuts the night before 'cuz the ground's covered with the stuff. It's bad enough they pee all over the place and leave their b.o. everywhere, they gotta break bottles, too.

Fatty then turns back to Africa and says, "Yo, you heard about Pete's house getting robbed, right?"

Africa looks up at Fatty, then at me, I guess to see whether Fatty's kidding or not. I always thought I had one of those mean poker faces, but I guess Africa can tell from one look that what Fatty said is true 'cuz he then says, "I'm sorry, Pete. That's messed up. I didn't know."

I don't say nothing 'cuz what the fuck is there to say? All I know is the last thing I need is some kid who's running all around for a goddamn nickel feeling sorry for me.

Of course, Fatty goes on yapping away, telling Africa about how everything got stolen right in broad daylight while Steven and me were at some stupid church picnic that my mom dragged us to. I guess Fatty got all the details from his mom, who's got an even bigger mouth than him and is into everyone's fucking business. With the two of them blabbing away, it's like I might as well be walking around with a sign. Pretty soon, everyone will know I got ripped off and ain't got no TV or Atari.

"And check it out, bro. 5-0 didn't do shit. They fucking dissed him right to his face."

"Give it a rest, Fatty."

"What's the big deal, bro? I'm just telling him what happened. Who knows, bro? Maybe Africa saw something."

Like I said before, I know better than to hope for stuff like that. But I can't help looking over at Africa anyway, just in case. I guess a part of me's still all stupid like that.

"I didn't see nothing, Pete," says Africa.

"Think hard, bro," says Fatty.

Africa just shakes his head.

"They probably wouldn't have carried his shit out in the open, bro. They probably hid it in boxes or bags so's people wouldn't know what they were up to."

"He said he didn't see nothing, Fatty," I half shout. But I might as well tell the kid to stop being fat or stupid.

"Come on, Africa. You were outside our building all day yesterday. You must have seen something."

Africa looks up at me and says, "I didn't see nothing, Pete. I swear. But you should talk to Jin. Maybe he saw something."

"Yo, where the hell is that kid anyway? He fucking owes me money," says Fatty.

Both me and Africa turn and stare at him for a while 'cuz neither of us can believe the cheap bastard actually lent anybody money.

"You lent Jin money?" I say.

"Hell yeah. And he better pay up, too, 'cuz 20 bucks is nothing compared to what I could do to that kid." He then goes on whining about what a cheap bastard Jin is.

I get sick of hearing him bellyaching like that 'cuz I hate whiners more than anything. So I turn around and look through the fence at some skinny little Spanish kid we never seen before rolling this garbage can underneath a basket to try to dunk.

All of a sudden, Fatty screams, "Holy shit! I got it!"

"Got what?" I say, turning back to him.

"I got it, bro. I know who housed your shit!"

I should know better than to ask 'cuz Fatty's the last person who'd figure out anything, but I can't help it. The son of a bitch just knows how to get you all worked up about things like that. So I say, "Who?" then regret it as soon as the word leaves my mouth.

"Haven't you figured it out yet, bro? You were standing right there."

"Right where?"

"I thought you were smart, bro. Don't they teach you nothing in the SP class?"

"What the fuck are you talking about, Fatty?"

"Damn, bro. Do I gotta spell out every little thing for you? Why d'you think those guys from the car wash were laughing so hard back there? It wasn't 'cuz of no stupid Pumas, bro. They were laughing their asses off 'cuz they housed your shit and you don't even know it."

I just stare at him, wondering how the hell he thinks the shit up.

"What?" he says.

"Just keep your mouth shut, all right. It's fucking embarrassing."

"Come on, bro. Why you gotta be like that for? I'm just going by the clues."

"Some guys laughing ain't no fucking clue."

"You're really gonna tell me you ain't even a little suspicious of those guys? I'm telling you, bro. My homeboy Quick told me they got these gangs of professional thieves from Brooklyn who make like movers with a truck and empty out houses. How much you wanna bet the car wash guys are in some gang like that?"

"Shut the fuck up."

Fatty turns to Africa and says, "Yo, Africa, did you see any moving trucks yesterday outside our building?"

Africa shakes his head. "I didn't see no moving truck."

"You sure?"

"Just drop it, Fatty. I'm not playing."

"Who says I'm playing, bro? I'm dead serious about looking for your shit. I'm even down to go check behind the car wash."

"We ain't checking shit. So just drop it, all right."

And I mean it. Whoever took my shit's probably sold it by now. So why am I gonna waste my time looking for shit that's already gone?

But Fatty just won't let it go. The bastard shakes his head and says, "I don't get it, bro. I figure a smart guy like you would be trying like crazy to get your shit back. It ain't even that hard, bro. All you gotta do is go around and talk to people and see if anyone saw anything. There's tons of people on our block, bro. One of 'em's gotta have seen something. Like that big-nosed Jew neighbor of yours. And Roman, too. That nigger lives right under you, don't he? Maybe he saw something."

"Fine, Fatty. You wanna play detective so bad? You go around asking people what they saw, all right? But leave me the hell out of it!"

"Damn, bro. What's your fucking problem? I'm just trying to help."

"I didn't ask for no help, all right. Anyway, what the fuck do you care? My apartment got robbed, not yours."

"I'm just watching your back. We're the Warriors, bro. The fucking Warriors."

"Just shut the fuck up, all right."

Fatty glares at me for a while like he's about to take a swing at me, then shrugs it off like nothing's the matter. That's the thing with Fatty. He'll act all pissed when you say shit to him, but he'll start grinning two seconds later like nothing just happened. It's like you can tell him right to his face that he's a fat worthless piece of shit who doesn't deserve to live and he'll just shrug and ask you if you wanna go get a Whopper.

All of a sudden, there's this loud clanging sound like a stack of pots just fell. So we look over and there's the little Spanish kid with the garbage can lying flat on his ass on the ground.

Right away, we drop what we're doing and rush over to the kid to make sure that he's okay. It's what we'd do to help any fellow human being 'cuz that's what they told us to do at school.

Get real.

Why do that when we can all stand there and start laughing our asses off like Heckle and Jeckle? 'Cuz there's nothing funnier than seeing some kid fall flat on his ass except maybe seeing two kids fall flat on their asses at the same time.

"That was awesome! Why don't you do it again!" Fatty shouts through the fence.

The kid looks up at us from the ground like he wants to shove a screwdriver right through our eyeballs.

"What's up? You got beef?"

The kid takes a second to size Fatty up, then keeps quiet. Not that I blame the kid. He looks like he barely comes up to Fatty's chest and maybe weighs about 60 pounds.

Then the kid gets up off the ground real slow, gets his ball, and walks away toward the sprinkler on the other side of the park.

"Thought so, stupidass!" Fatty shouts after the kid, puffing out his chest like he just had a real fight. I kind of feel sorry for the little kid, but then again, it's not like Fatty hit him or nothing.

If that had happened, the kid better have fought back. 'Cuz it don't matter how big the other guy is, you don't ever just stand there and do nothing when someone hits you. You gotta fight and prove you got heart. Otherwise, you might as well throw in the towel and be a doormat for the rest of your life 'cuz that's all you'll ever be, a fucking doormat like Hindu Tim.

I don't know if that's what the little kid's thinking, but when he's about 20 yards away, he turns around and shouts, "Fuck you, you fatass! Go on a fucking diet!"

Me and Africa start laughing real loud. It's not that what the kid said was even that funny or that we're instigating, but you gotta hand it to the kid for having the guts to say something.

Fatty turns red and screams, "You're dead, you little fuck. You're fucking dead!"

The little kid just gives Fatty the finger, then runs outta the park.

If it were some other day, we might go after the kid, but the kid's too fast and it's too damn hot so we don't even bother. Why do that when we know we're bound to run into the kid again sooner or later 'cuz where the hell's the kid gonna go? That's the thing with trying to run from someone. You might get away for a while, even for weeks or months, but you can't run forever.

"Warriors are faggots!" someone shouts from behind us.

We turn around and see Diego standing in front of the blue square on the far wall. The ugly, useless dickhead points a home-made stickball bat, a ratty old broomstick with some electrical tape wrapped around the bottom, right at us and says, "What's up, you little homos? Eat any dogs today? I heard some lady on our block's looking for her Chihuahua!"

Me, Fatty, and Africa just look at each other and shake our heads. It's like today's Start With the Warriors Day or something. We've been outside for less than an hour and every douchebag in town's started with us for no reason just like how that sheriff and his gang of dickheads did to John Rambo before they got what was coming to them.

Anyway, we ain't about to let the asshole just dis us like that and do nothing, so I shout back, "No, man. But your mother did. When she was sucking my dick last night!"

Diego grabs his balls with one hand and gives me the finger with the other. "Fuck you, Stitch!"

I give him the finger right back. I so want to wipe the grin off the bastard's face, and not just 'cuz he called me by that name or 'cuz he's been talking shit about how I throw.

So I turn to Africa. And the kid holds up a tennis ball. What can you say? It's like the kid can read my mind.

CHAPTER 4

S T-R-I-I-I-KE ONE!"
Fatty makes like an ump as soon as the ball bounces off the middle of the blue square.

Diego kicks the ball back at me, then taps his bat on the bottom of his shelltops like he's some superstar about to send the ball out of the park.

I snag the ball off the ground and give it a couple of bounces. The ball's just the way I like 'em, brand new with hardly no fuzz.

I put my fingers on the rubber seams, then look over at the sideline, where there's a whole bunch of kids, like they fucking popped up from out of the ground.

I turn back to the blue square. Diego gives me the evil eye and tries to psych me out, but I don't pay him no mind. He's never been much of a hitter, even though he goes around telling people that Reggie Jackson's his uncle. It's about the dumbest lie I've ever heard. I don't even like the Yankees, and I know Mr. October's a superstar, who hit three home runs in three swings in the World Series and should never have been traded to the fucking Angels, while Diego's a loser, a spic, and a bullshit artist, whose dad mops up the hallway, takes out the garbage, and steals stuff off us kids for no reason.

Just thinking about the fucking super leaves a bad taste in my mouth. But I focus and collect myself 'cuz that's what you gotta do when you pitch, stay cool, like Jesse Orosco when he comes in and gets one save after another with his killer sliders.

So I take a deep breath and throw my second pitch. It's high, but Diego swings anyway and misses by more than two feet. It's like he's not even looking at the ball.

Still, the douchebag's gotta play it off like he's some bigshot, so he shouts, "The next one's outta here, man! Stickball's not for fucking chinos!"

I smile as cool as can be. The son of a bitch can say whatever he wants. He can call me "chino." He can tell me to open my eyes and go back to China. He can "ching-chong" me to death and tell me to go eat pork fried rice and say how I'm all mixed up 'cuz my mom's Chinese and my dad's Japanese and call me every name in the book. It don't matter none 'cuz there ain't nothing he can say that I haven't heard and I just don't give a fuck.

The only thing that matters is that I'm ahead in the count and about to strike his ass out in front of the whole park. Of course, you know the bastard will come up with a thousand and one excuses why he couldn't hit the ball, but we'll both know I struck his ass out fair and square.

My third pitch is the best and zips to the wall so fast that it's just a blur of a blur. Like I said before, I don't have a radar gun or anything, but it's at least a hundred miles per hour, if not faster.

The only thing is, Diego swings and somehow manages to connect. I don't know if it's the sound his bat makes or just seeing the bat hit the ball, but I know instantly that it's out of there. I don't even have to look. But I do anyway and see it clear the fence by more than 20 feet. I can't help it. I'm all sick like that.

Africa and Fatty rush over to me, to try to make me feel better, I guess. But the looks on their faces just make me feel worse.

"Forget it, Pete. It don't mean nothing. He just got lucky," says Africa.

It ain't true. So I just stand there as Diego swaggers up to me, swinging the stickball bat in front of him like it's some machete and he's making his way through some coconut jungle. Forget being a good sport and all that. I know the jerkoff's gonna rub it in my face. If the tables were turned, I'd do the exact same thing.

The douchebag comes right up to me and says, "Like I said before, man. Stickball's not for chinos. When are you gonna figure that out?"

"Fuck you. You just got lucky."

"Luck, my ass." He then turns to Africa and says, "Yo, you lost, man. Now pay up."

I look over at Africa 'cuz I have no idea what the fuck Diego's talking about. But Africa gives me this look like everything's cool and he's gonna handle it. He then takes out a pack of jumping jacks from the crumpled-up brown paper bag he always carries around.

Diego shakes his head and says, "The whole bag, man."

"But I said just one pack."

"Stop lying. You said all of them. Now give it up!"

"But I said . . ."

"I said give it up." Diego shoves Africa hard in the chest with both hands and sends him back a good three feet.

And just like that, all eyes turn to Africa and everything gets real quiet like someone just killed the sound on the TV.

Me and everyone there wait for Africa to start swinging 'cuz if you've ever been in a fight, you know that nine times out of ten, whoever swings first wins, and the only reason the tenth kid doesn't is 'cuz someone breaks it up. But Africa doesn't do a damn thing. He just stands there with this scared look on his face like he's about to crap his pants.

"What the fuck you waiting for, bro? Kick his ass," says Fatty.

"Yeah, man. Kick his ass!" some other kid shouts.

But Africa just goes on doing nothing, then looks down at the ground, like he's hoping Diego will just go away by magic when he looks back up.

Some kid behind me lets out a groan. It's like when you light a firecracker and it turns out to be a dud. It's almost as bad as Hindu Tim, who'll sometimes fall down on the ground crying before anyone even touches him.

Then, with the whole park looking on, Diego goes up to Africa and snatches the bag of jumping jacks right out of his hands.

"Thought so," he says, then turns around and starts walking away like nothing just happened and he didn't just mug Africa.

From behind me, someone says, "What a chickenshit!"

There's all this laughing and Africa's head drops even lower. I don't know what to do or say. I mean, Africa's my homeboy and all that and we're both part of the Warriors, but he can't go around acting like some scared little kid, especially not when someone takes your shit. It don't matter whether it's a bike or a penny

Swedish fish, you don't just stand there and let someone snatch your shit from you no matter how scared you are or how much your knees are shaking.

Anyway, I can't look at Africa no more without getting disgusted. So I turn and stare at Diego, who's walking out the park. The dickweed's huge and has no neck. The only kid who's fatter in our grade's some commie Yugoslavian kid named Atlas Abicic, who's got tits bigger than most of the girls and will let you slap him hard in the face for 50 cents 'cuz all the nerves there are dead from some weird car accident he had when he was little.

The next thing I know, I'm running right at the son of a bitch, screaming at the top of my lungs. And by the time the bastard turns his head to look at me, it's too late. I dive right at the back of his knees and he goes down like a sack of garbage.

CHAPTER 5

"KILL THAT PUNK!" someone shouts.

Who knows who they mean. Except for Fatty, Africa, and Steven, no one could care less who kicks whose ass. All they want is a free show. And if there's blood or a broken bone, so much the better.

Not that I blame them. I'd much rather watch two kids trying to kill each other than some stupid TV show any day, too, unless it's the drive-in movie, the *Benny Hill Show*, or the Italian sex movies they sometimes got on channel 13 late at night. My favorite's this one where a snooty rich lady gets stuck on this island in the middle of nowhere with some servant guy and they start doing it all over the place. I know I gotta sound like some horny little kid, but I must have jerked off to that movie a fucking hundred times. But then again, I even jerk off to *Wonder Woman*, so it doesn't take a lot to get me all excited.

Anyway, Diego gets up off the floor and tries to grab my arm, but I slide out of the way and kick him hard in the shin 'cuz if we start wrestling, then I'm dead.

So I start swinging. And he starts swinging, which is hilarious 'cuz the bastard punches just like he plays stickball, swinging wildly for home runs. Still, he lands a couple of shots that I actually feel, which means they're some serious punches, 'cuz usually you don't feel shit when you fight.

I don't know how much time goes by. But when both of us are dead tired and huffing and puffing, Diego picks up his broomstick off the ground and comes charging at me. Sure, it's sneaky. But he's Puerto Rican, so I can't really blame him. It's in his genes. Fact is, the only good Puerto Rican I ever knew was Roman, and he's half black.

Anyway, the bat comes swinging right down at my head, but I raise my left arm just in time, so it hits my forearm and snaps in half.

Something about the bat breaking like that must have freaked the dickhead out 'cuz he just stands there for a moment like he's in some kind of daze, which's the dumbest thing you can do in a fight. And to teach him that valuable lesson, I take a step toward him and kick him hard right in the nuts. It's like I'm kicking a field goal except the ball never goes through the uprights, but just goes *CRUNCH!*

I never took no karate or tae kwon do, and I definitely never did no wax on wax off for no bow-legged Jap bastard, but I still must have done some serious damage 'cuz Diego's mouth opens into the letter O and he drops to his knees as if in slow motion. What's left of the busted bat slips out of his hand, and he looks up at me like some helpless spic rat.

For a full second, I actually stop and wonder if I've killed the bastard. But then I pull myself together and punch him right in the nose. If it were a drive-in movie, blood would start bubbling out his mouth and he'd take five minutes to keel over and die.

But we ain't in no movie, and I ain't no one-armed fighter wandering around China with no flying guillotine. So Diego doesn't bite it.

But all this blood does start gushing out his nose in buckets and drips down the entire front of his shirt. Some kid runs over and tells him to put his head back to stop the bleeding. Some other kid runs over and says don't 'cuz all that does is make the blood go down your throat.

Fuck if I care. The bastard and his dad probably sit around and drink chicken blood 'cuz you know all Puerto Ricans do voodoo even though they pretend to be all into God and the Virgin Mary and all that.

Fatty rushes over to me and lifts my arm high in the air like I'm Rocky and he's the old guy who played the Penguin. Not that anyone's wondering who kicked whose ass. A whole bunch of kids crowd around me and tap my shoulder and back to tell me I done good. For every single one of them, this will be the highlight of their day. They'll all go off to their blocks and tell their friends how a skinny little Chinese kid beat up a fat Puerto Rican kid twice his size with a mean five-deadly-venoms kick to the balls.

Three Spanish kids help Diego up and start walking him outta the park. I must have really hurt the asshole bad 'cuz he doesn't even think to make like he ain't hurt. If I'da got my ass kicked, I'd be running around with my arms raised saying, "And I'll kick your ass again next time, too!" just to make the other kid think I was crazy. But Diego just trudges away without saying nothing.

Steven comes over to me and holds up Africa's bag of jumping jacks. I guess the kid must have picked it up while Diego and me were fighting.

I take the bag from him and try to give it to Africa.

But he won't take it. He just keeps saying, "No, Pete. You keep it."

I shake my head no and push the bag into his hand.

But he just lets it drop on the ground. Some kid. He won't fight a guy who just mugged him in front of everybody, but he's gotta make like he's got his pride.

Of course, Fatty, who couldn't give a rat's ass about pride, runs over and grabs the bag in half a second, then says, "Yo, Africa. You sure you don't want this?"

"Keep it."

"Don't ask for it back later 'cuz I ain't gonna give it back."

Africa doesn't say nothing.

I turn back to Diego, who's staring at me with daggers from 50 yards away.

"This isn't over, man. I'm gonna get my cousin after you! You're fucking dead, you fucking chino! You hear me! You're fucking dead!"

I can't believe how pathetic the son of a bitch sounds. You know when a kid tells you his backup is his cousin that you ain't got a damn thing to worry about 'cuz the kid's a complete pussy and the cousin's probably an even bigger pussy. So I really shouldn't even bother saying nothing back. But I can't help myself. What can I say? I like to kick people when they're down.

So I say, "Go ahead, you faggot. Get your cousin! I'll kick his ass, too!"

Diego flips me the bird.

Me and Fatty return the favor. Then Fatty shouts, "That's

what you get for messing with us, you fuck! You mess with the Warriors, you mess with your life!" He then holds up both his arms and screams, "Can you dig it! Can you dig it!"

Standing there next to Fatty, who's all pumped up like it was him who just fought and not me, it hits me just how weird things can be sometimes. I mean, I can't really say I fought Diego 'cuz of the Warriors or for Africa, but kicking his ass in front of the whole park should make me feel awesome. But that's the farthest from what I really feel. And it's not just 'cuz my right eye is numb and my arm hurts like crazy, neither. I've gone through stuff that hurt a hundred times worse. It's that I have this creepy feeling like when the two guys go hide out in that church in *The Outsiders,* which is the only book I ever read where white kids weren't complete pussies. What did the guy call it? A premonition? It's exactly the same feeling I had when Dad sent me to Dr. Min last summer, which I'll tell you about later.

"Yo, what's that in your knee, bro?" says Fatty.

I look down at where Fatty's pointing. And just like that, even though I didn't feel a thing there just a second ago, now that I see the piece of glass wedged right in the middle of my knee, it suddenly hurts like crazy. The entire leg feels like it's on fire, like someone cut me with a knife and started rubbing salt and lemon juice all over it.

Still, I gotta play it off like it ain't no big deal, so I try not to wince and just say, "Shit."

Of course, good old Fatty just has to ask, "Yo, does it hurt?"

It's like when geniuses see you with a cast on your arm, then ask you if you broke your arm. No, you fuck. It doesn't hurt at all. I put the glass in my knee on purpose 'cuz it fucking makes me feel good. Goddamn!

CHAPTER 6

YOU MIGHT FIGURE that a little bruise above the eye or a piece of glass in the knee should be nothing for a kid who's had the world's most painful operation, but that's another weird thing about me. I go around acting like I got guts, but I just can't take no pain. So I can't help cringing as I wash my knee out with water from some hydrant that someone forgot to turn off all the way.

Not that I'm whining, 'cuz I hate fucking whiners more than I hate spics and chinks. But if my luck continues the way it has, my knee will probably get infected and gangrene will set in. Then I'll have to bite down on a stick while Fatty or Africa cleans it out with a burning knife like in that movie where the guy escapes from prison only to have these greedy nuns steal his pearls and turn him over to the cops.

"You all right, Pete?"

I turn around and see Africa standing behind me. The kid's sort of like Steven that way. They both got this way of sneaking up on you all quiet like they're fucking ninjas or something.

"I'm all right," I say.

He shifts from one foot to the other like he's all nervous, then says, "I guess I was a real chickenshit back there, huh?"

He was, but I ain't gonna say that 'cuz what good would that do? So I just say, "Forget it. It gave me a good excuse to kick Diego's ass."

"I just don't know what's wrong with me these days, Pete. I wanted to swing. I really did. I just couldn't. I guess I just don't have heart anymore."

"It ain't no big deal. He was bigger than you."

"He was bigger than you, too. I should have fought him, not you."

I don't say nothing 'cuz Africa's right and we both know it.

And nothing any of us says now's gonna change the fact that a part of me will always wonder from now on whether he can really be counted on for backup.

"It's all my fault. I shouldn't have bet him from the beginning. But he made such a stupid bet, I couldn't pass it up."

"Just forget the whole thing, all right, Africa. It ain't no big deal."

"You think Diego's really gonna get his cousin after you?"

"Who knows? He probably doesn't even have a cousin," I say, then shake the water off my hands.

Africa just stands there with this look like he's about to go down to the railroad tracks and jump in front of the train, which is another reason why he should have fought. That way, even if he got his ass kicked, at least he wouldn't feel so damn bad about himself.

I know it's weird, but even though Africa's all depressed like that, I can't help but laugh a little 'cuz of how funny looking he is. His skin's all dark and shit like all he ever does is sit out in the sun, even though summer's just started and none of us has yet to go to the beach or the five-cent pool. Not that that's why we call him Africa even though that makes sense, too.

We call him that 'cuz that's where he was born. Why anyone would go to Africa from Korea makes no sense to me, but no one said Africa's parents were geniuses. All I know is they got kicked out of fucking Africa right after Africa was born.

Anyway, I put him in a fake headlock just to horse around and get him laughing again 'cuz the last thing I want is to have him go around with this hangdog expression on his face all day.

It seems to work a little, and the guy actually smiles as we walk back to Fatty, who's sitting on some bench near the swings, where a bunch of little girls with no tits are giggling about something stupid.

"I think those girls like you, Fatty," I say, just to mess with him a little.

He makes like he didn't hear me, then says, "I don't know how you do it, bro."

I don't know what the hell he's talking about until he points with his chin to Steven, who's crouched on the ground near the sprinklers, which is shooting water 20 feet in the air even though there's supposed to be a drought and they're telling everyone to save water all the time. All around him, a bunch of little kids are screaming and splashing around in their underwear, not giving a damn that the whole world can see their buttcracks right through their Fruit of the Looms.

It's like Steven doesn't even see them. He's just sitting there, staring at a couple of empty soda cans like they were the most interesting things in the world. The kid's all weird like that. He'll zone out like that every now and then and focus on the weirdest fucking things. Like sometimes, all he'll do at home is sit down and spend hours counting all these thousands of pennies that he's picked up off the ground and keeps in these kimchi jars.

"I just don't know how the hell you do it, bro," says Fatty. "If I had a little weirdo brother I had to babysit all the time, I'd go fucking crazy."

It ain't that I disagree with Fatty. I just don't need him to tell me Steven's weird. I already know that. And I've thought about ditching the kid lots of times. Not that what I do with him's exactly babysitting. It's more like I let him tag along just enough so that Mom doesn't get on my case. Not that I feel guilty about it or anything. The kid's gotta learn to get by on his own just the way I did. Otherwise, he's gonna grow up to be a fucking wuss like Hindu Tim, who gets picked on by everybody even though he's got a beard and looks like he should be sitting behind the counter of some Optimo selling cheap cigars.

Still, it bugs the shit out of me that Fatty's bad-mouthing someone in my family. I mean, who the hell is he to talk? So his dad's got some fish store that makes a lot of money. Big fucking deal. His dad's almost a midget, who ain't much bigger than us kids. And his mom talks Korean with a thick farmer accent like she just stepped off some rice paddy, which she probably did. Both of them are from some real hick town in Korea where pigs run around everywhere eating shit and people wipe their asses with crumpled-up newspapers.

So I look right at the bastard and say, "If you had a little brother, Fatty, he'd go crazy before you."

It takes a few seconds for Fatty to figure out that he's just been dissed. When he finally does, he says, "But I don't have a little brother, bro. You do."

That's about the stupidest comeback in the book. He might as well tell me he's rubber and I'm glue and you know the rest. It'd even be better if he kept his mouth shut and just ripped one.

Of course, Fatty ain't at all bothered at how stupid his comeback was. He just takes out his marker from the back pocket of his shorts and starts making a big show of shaking it up to get the ink going just to look cool in front of the flat-chested girls checking us out from the swings.

Then he starts tagging up on the back of the bench next to where some wiseass's already scribbled, *"SAVE WATER. DON'T TAKE NO SHOWERS!"*

But instead of writing *"WARRIORS"* or *"FATTY"* as he usually does, Fatty writes *"SUMO."*

"What the hell's *sumo?"* I say.

"What d'you think it is? It's my new tag, bro."

"Sumo?"

"At least it's better than *Stitch,"* he says.

I shoot him this look that says I'm not kidding around and say, "How many times I gotta tell you not to call me that? I'm not fucking playing around, Fatty."

"All right, all right. Calm the fuck down. I was just kidding. Anyway, you like my new tag, right? It's fucking dope, ain't it?" he says, putting the marker back in his pocket.

"How long did it take you to think that up?" I say, all sarcastic.

"I didn't think it up. My homeboy Quick gave me that tag. That's how tags work, bro. You don't just make 'em up. You gotta earn 'em. With heart and blood. Like a badge of courage. That's how I got *Nato Sabe* back in the day."

"You don't write *Nato Sabe*. So don't even bullshit about it."

"Hell yeah, I do. I started writing *Nato Sabe* when I was seven years old. That's when I first started going to the graveyard and running from Larry and Curly."

"Bullshit."

"I ain't lying, bro. I'll bet you a hundred dollars it's all true."

I ain't in no mood to make no stupid bet with Fatty. Even if I won, the kid would just welsh out of it, so why fucking bother? Fact is, he may talk a whole bunch of shit about what a badass tagger he is and how he climbs over razor-sharp barbed-wire fences to tag up on trains and how he almost got caught all these times by the cops, but in truth, he ain't done shit except scribble on some walls with markers. If you ask me, his best tag so far was writing *"A crazy lady lives here"* on the side of the Leben Home.

Compared to Fatty, Nato Sabe's bigtime. He's up all over the place, on trains, on the sides of buildings, on rooftops, everywhere. None of us know who he is, but if I had to make a bet, I'd bet it's probably some corny whiteboy 'cuz that's just how it is. Black kids rap and breakdance. And whiteboys tag up, at least they do if they ain't complete fucking nerds.

Take Maspeth, for example, which is this whiteboy neighborhood on the other side of Queens Boulevard where all of us would be going to school if the Holland had been on the other side of the street instead of where it is. Not that I think it makes much of a difference where we go to school. The teachers would still suck and try to tell you what to do all the time. And all of us would still be labeled troublemakers with serious attitude problems. The only difference is, at Maspeth, we'd be fighting crazy whiteboys instead of spics and crazy black kids from the projects and we'd maybe get to mess around with horny white girls, who everyone knows are the biggest sluts. Just look in any porno if you don't believe me. The point is, you won't ever hear or see nothing in Maspeth but crazy metalhead whiteboys, who get stoned out of their minds and drive around looking for little kids to jump 'cuz they're all fucking pussies at heart. But you'll still see all this graffiti all over the place, which just goes to show that rap and graffiti ain't the same thing.

Anyway, Fatty goes on and says, "Quick gave me the tag 'cuz he saw me fight this big black guy who was trying to steal hot sauce from my dad's store. I chased that nigger down three blocks and punched him right in his eyes. Gave that sucker two black eyes." He pauses. "Get it? I gave a black guy black eyes."

Africa and me just shake our heads. For a kid who's supposedly all crazy into rap, scratching, and breakdancing, it's amazing how corny Fatty can be sometimes. I mean, it'd be even better if he just told us knock-knock jokes and shit.

Of course, none of that bugs Fatty at all. He just says, "Quick said I had guts. Said I'm tough like a sumo master. You guys know what sumo is, right?"

"Yeah," I say. "It's this wrestling they do in Japan where they wear diapers."

Fatty gives me this real phony laugh and says, "Good one, bro. Real funny. Maybe you'll make someone laugh next time."

"Look, Fatty. You don't gotta lie to us all the time," I say.

"I ain't lying."

"Come on, Fatty. You really expect us to believe that you beat up some big black guy? After how tough you were back at the car wash?"

"I don't expect nothing, bro. It's a free country. You can believe whatever you want. All I'm gonna say is, I don't need to impress you punks. So why am I gonna make this shit up for?"

"You tell us, Fatty."

He shakes his head like we just called his mom a five-dollar prostitute and says, "The hell with yous, bro. I don't know why you're always doubting me for no reason. I mean, have I ever once lied to you about anything?"

Africa and me look at each other. Not that we even have to think about it. Then we both say, "Yeah, Fatty. All the time."

"Name one time. Just one time. I dare you."

"Fine, Fatty," I say. "How 'bout the time at school when you told everybody that you're related to the president of Korea?"

"I am."

"You ain't related to no president."

"Hell yeah, I am. Not the president now, but the first president of Korea."

"Come on, Fatty. Just listen to yourself."

"You don't believe me? I'll bet you a hundred dollars. You can even look it up in the encyclopedia. We can go to the library and check it out right now. His last name was Rhee, just like mine."

"Big fucking deal, Fatty. You know how many people have that last name?"

"But they ain't related to him. I am. I'm not kidding around, bro. He's my mom's uncle. You can even go ask her. She'll tell you what's what."

"You're full of shit."

"I ain't bullshitting you, bro. I swear to God."

"Fine, Fatty. How 'bout the time you said your dad makes a million dollars a year?"

"He does."

"Your dad don't make no million dollars."

"Sure, he does. In fact, he makes more than that, but I didn't wanna seem like I was bragging. Truth is, he makes closer to two million, but he don't tell that to the government 'cuz of taxes."

"Your dad makes two million dollars a year?"

"Yeah."

"Come on, Fatty."

"I swear, bro. I'm not making this up. I swear on my grand-mother's grave. I wouldn't lie about this stuff, bro."

"Then how come your family still lives here, hunh? Why don't your dad buy you some big house out on Long Island or Jersey?"

He's quiet for a second like he's thinking of something to say, then says, "He could do that in a second if he wanted to. But we like it here. So why're we gonna move for?"

"Stop lying."

"How can I stop something that I ain't doing? I'm telling you the truth, bro. You've never been to my dad's store. You should see how they line up around the block at lunchtime. Black people love fried fish. I'm telling you, bro. If you wanna make money, you gotta have a store in a black neighborhood. White people are cheap, bro. And they're all fucking prejudiced. Everyone knows that."

"Fine, Fatty. So your mom's uncle was president and your dad makes two million dollars a year."

"You can believe me or not, bro. That's up to you. Tell you the truth, it don't matter to me none what you think. 'Cuz what's important is that I know. And God knows." He then tilts his head back and looks up at the sky like he's looking right at God and God's looking down right at him. What can you say? The kid just cracks me up sometimes. He'll act like he's all into God or something even though he's the biggest fucking klepto on the block and shoots cats with his BB gun for fun and his mom goes to see some crazy Korean fortune-teller in Flushing who dances around with knives and claims to tell the future by squeezing people's pimples.

"Damn, Fatty. You think God's got nothing better to do than keep track of all the lies you tell?"

Fatty gives me a phony laugh, then says, "Real funny, bro. Keep it up and we'll see what happens later."

"I'm so scared. What are you gonna do? Kick my ass like you did all those big black guys?"

"Just keep it up, bro. And you'll find out. That's all I'm gonna say for now."

"What you gonna do? Do Tiger Chung Lee on me?"

"That ain't funny, bro."

"What? That's your master's name, ain't it? Tiger Chung Lee?"

"That ain't my master's name." He glares at me. The next thing you know the bastard'll tell me I've dishonored his master, then we'll fight to the death on some fucking cliff.

"Tiger whatever. Tae kwon do's garbage and you know it."

It's not that Fatty and me mean to rag on each other all the time. It's just how we make the time go sometimes 'cuz there just ain't that much to do other than walk around from one place to another or mess with the nut jobs who wander out from the Leben Home. Sure, once in a while we'll spend all day making something out of the junk we find lying around. Like this one time, we built a go-cart out of all these old shopping carts and busted bicycles we found. Of course, the go-cart didn't look so sharp like the ones you see in the back of comic books. But considering that the only tools we had were a rusty plier and half a brick, which we used as a hammer, it really wasn't that bad. And we had fun zooming down this hill next to the Leben Home. The only thing is we never put no brakes on the damn thing, so all of us ended up crashing head-on into this parked car. Still, it was fun as hell. But those kinds of days are hard to come by. Fact is, most days go by so fucking slow that a single day can seem to stretch on forever.

Anyway, Fatty's quiet for a while, which means he's either hungry or about to cut one, then says, "Yo, what d'you guys say we go to the movies later? They got this movie at the Colony that's got a hundred naked girls with tits out to here!"

He holds up his hands in front of his chest and starts laughing, making his stomach jiggle like Jell-O and his already beady eyes all but disappear.

"I heard they even got this scene where this naked girl rides a horse and her titties bounce up and down in slow motion, bro."

It ain't that I don't like horses or naked girls with big bouncing tits. I got eyes, hormones, and needs like any other kid, which means I'm thinking about sex nearly all the time, even when I'm sleeping. But I just don't feel like sitting around the Colony for some reason. And it ain't 'cuz of the sticky floors there or the rip that runs down nearly the entire left side of the screen.

I don't know. Maybe it's getting my stuff ripped off or just how damn hot it is, but I don't much feel like doing anything. Anyway, even if I did, I'm broke, so how the hell am I gonna come up with two bucks for the ticket? God knows, Fatty, who's worse than Scrooge, ain't gonna hook me up.

But then, Fatty says, "You don't need no money, bro. The guy who checks tickets goes to my tae kwon do school. He can get us in for free. Even your little brother."

"I don't know, Fatty."

"Come on, bro. What else are we gonna do? Play fucking kick-the-can?"

"Goddamn, Fatty. I said I don't know. If you wanna go so bad, go already."

He smiles all perverted and says, "Come on, bro. My friend says there's this girl who hangs out in the lobby, who gives blowjobs for five bucks."

The other thing about Fatty is he's always going on and on about all these girls he knows who'll do all kinds of super sexy stuff for five bucks. He also claims to have gotten a blowjob in the Mets Motel parking lot and swears on everything you can think of that he did it last summer with some girl in Korea who gave up her virginity for his Walkman, which wasn't even a real Sony, but some crappy knock-off from Chinatown. I know it's all bullshit, but the way he tells it, with a straight face and without ever blinking or nothing, the bastard has this way of making it sound so damn real.

Anyway, just when I'm about to call him on his bullshit, he says, "Yo, ain't that your dad?"

I turn to where he's looking and see my dad sitting around with a whole bunch of old ajussies. All of them are wearing the standard ajussy uniform, white tank tops from Korea and two-dollar flip-flops, with cigarettes or toothpicks sticking out their mouths, talking bullshit and reading the Korean newspaper, which's gotta be the most worthless rag ever. It's 'cuz of that bullshit waste of paper and ink that I had to go through what I did with my operation.

Anyway, just seeing my dad like that makes me sick. He should be out working, making money for our family. Instead, he's sitting around with losers doing nothing while Mom's killing herself hemming pants and fixing zippers and working so much that she's going blind and all her hair's turning gray even though she's only 45.

One thing's for sure. When I grow up, I ain't never gonna have my wife work like a dog while I sit around on my ass all day. You can bet anything that I'm gonna make sure I'm making money somehow. I'll even collect cans if I have to. Shit, I'll even rob banks if I have to. But there's no way in hell my kid's gonna see me sitting around being a fucking bum.

So I start walking outta there, but he sees me and yells for me to come over with Steven. That's the thing with the guy. I don't know if it's from growing up in the country, but he's got fucking amazing eyesight.

Anyway, if I had B.J.'s guts, I'd tell him to drop dead or go get a job, but I don't. So me and Steven start walking over to him real slow like we're walking the plank.

Knowing Dad, he's probably gonna tell me something stupid like keep an eye on Steven or look both ways before crossing the street. I wish the guy would just leave me alone. Either that or find a different park to be a bum in. I mean, of all the goddamn parks in the world, why's he gotta hang out in mine for? You don't see Fatty's dad or Africa's dad sitting around doing nothing, do you?

CHAPTER 7

EVER SINCE DAD almost got killed by these black guys this time he got lost in Brooklyn somewhere, he's been real scared to drive by himself, which is why he used to have me go with him to buy supplies for his store.

This one time, right after we cross the Williamsburg Bridge, Dad makes this left turn all of a sudden right in front of where there's this huge *"NO LEFT TURN"* sign and where this cop car's parked right across the street.

The cop pulls us over and starts giving us this long lecture about how there's a hundred accidents right in that intersection and what the hell are we thinking pulling a move like that. Of course, Dad just smiles at the guy, then tells me to ask him not to give us a ticket 'cuz he couldn't understand the no-left-turn-sign 'cuz he doesn't know English. That's the kind of stuff Dad has me do for him all the time.

The only thing is, I can't do it 'cuz the sign isn't even written in English. It's just this picture, an arrow pointing left with a slash through it. But Dad keeps giving me this look like I'm letting down our entire family, so I finally give in and ask the cop what Dad wants. Not that it makes any difference 'cuz the cop just shakes his head and says, "Tell your father I can't do that."

The way that cop said it, though, you'd think we'd asked him to shoot a dozen dogs for us for fun or something.

Dad grumbled at me for the rest of that day like the whole thing was somehow my fault. But what the hell was I supposed to do? Get down on my knees and beg the cop to let us slide? Some things you just can't talk your way out of.

Anyway, I don't know why, but I keep thinking about that time as I stand there in front of Dad's pathetic old-men club.

Dad rubs my head, which I absolutely hate, then says, "What happened to your eye?"

I stare right at the ground and say, "I fell."

He doesn't buy it, but doesn't press me on it, either. That's the thing with Dad. I don't know if it's 'cuz Mom and him had me and Steven when they were so old, which is why they look about 20 years older than Fatty and Africa's parents and are always telling me and Steven how we should get married and have kids as soon as we grow up. But he's always giving me way too much benefit of the doubt. Like the time he got called down to the Woolworth's 'cuz I got caught stealing watches. I told him the store made a mistake and I just forgot to pay for it, which is gotta be about the most pathetic lie in the book, but he actually believed me and even yelled at the manager in Korean. I guess he just couldn't believe that his own son could be capable of something so crummy like that. Not that I'm bragging, but Mom and Dad have gotta be the squarest fucking people ever. I doubt they ever swiped anything off of anybody in their entire fucking lives.

Anyway, one of the old bastards, who looks like he's the club president, then turns to Dad and says, "You never told us your boy's the mirror image of you."

Dad smiles, and a couple of the old bastards say yeah, he is, which's a crock of shit 'cuz Dad looks Filipino or like he's mixed, which he might be 'cuz he's an orphan and doesn't know who his parents were, and which is why when he first started his store in the subway station, the other Korean people in the stores next to him left him alone. That's the thing with Korean people. They're all so fucking prejudiced.

Anyway, all the old bastards around us make a big fuss over me and Steven like they ain't never seen no kids before. It's like we're monkeys in some circus and they're all lined up to throw peanuts at us except all of them are too cheap and poor for peanuts.

I hate every single one of them. They all look beat and have bad teeth and smell old and sick like they're all about to keel over and die any second. Every single one of them's at least 20 years older than Dad, so who knows why he hangs out with them.

All I can do is stand there and ready myself for one of them to talk my ear off about the Korean War and how everyone back then had to eat leaves, sleep in caves, and dive for cover whenever a plane flew by and how we kids are super lucky in comparison so we should all be thankful.

But there's no story. Not even a half story or some old bastard whining about the good old days.

Instead, some old geezer, whose skin looks like a chewed-up baseball glove, rubs my head and says, in Korean, "So you're the boy who does so well in school. Good for you, kiddo. Keep it up and show everyone how smart we Koreans can be. You show them what sort of family you come from."

I don't know what Dad's been telling them about me, but none of it's true. Sure, I used to get okay grades back in P.S. 13, but that's all ancient history. Fact is, my grades have been falling quickly and steadily at an alarming rate ever since I got to junior high, and I barely passed this year by a couple of points. Of course, there's a lot of reasons for that—my parents getting a divorce, my favorite grandmother passing away suddenly from a stroke, my dog Master Killer getting run over by a truck, my girlfriend Grace getting gunned down in cold blood by the cops for jaywalking, all the teachers at 233 being card-carrying members of the KKK, and Steven getting diagnosed with incurable leukemia—but none of them's true. The real reason is that school's boring as shit and the teachers couldn't give a crap and they never teach you nothing interesting.

The same geezer's about to say something else, but I've had enough of his bullshit and I can't take it no more. So I shout, "What the fuck do you care, you old fart? You're just some old guy who ain't even related to us! So shut the fuck up."

At least that's what I should do. Instead, I just nod and stand there while the old fogey messes up my hair again.

Then I turn to Dad and say, in Korean, "Can we go now?"

"Wait a second, Minho," he says. The sound of my Korean name makes me want to puke. I don't know who Minho is, but it sounds like he's some super loser who brings kimchi to school and stinks up the entire lunchroom, has buck teeth, a rice-bowl haircut, and bows to all his teachers. Not that I got anything against Korean kids. They're all right, I guess. But I just wish they weren't all fucking losers, that's all.

I mean, Fatty, Africa, Jin, and me are all right 'cuz we're from the Holland and we know what's up. But you should see some of the other Korean kids at school. I don't know what planet they're from, but how the hell they became such fucking goody-goodys is beyond me. They all think we're fucking crazy delinquents just 'cuz we ain't wusses and actually talk back to the teachers every now and then. Like the time we all showed up for Mr. Schulman's English class with rolls of toilet paper instead of notebooks 'cuz that's what the corny teacher joked we could do the day before. All the other Korean kids acted like we should be sent to Riker's.

Anyway, Dad hands me an envelope and says, "This came in the mail. Tell me what it says."

I don't have to read it. It's just some stupid phony junk mail telling him that he may have already won ten million dollars if he subscribes to a half dozen magazines. So I tell him that. "It's nothing, Dad. They just want you to buy magazines."

But he won't listen to me, which drives me crazy 'cuz he's the one who asked me to read it for him.

He just makes this *tsk, tsk* sound with his tongue like all Korean people do, then says, "Don't be in such a rush. Read it carefully and tell me what it says. It says ten million dollars on the envelope, doesn't it?"

That's another thing with Dad. He's always asking all these rhetorical questions, which just drives me mad 'cuz I'm starting to do it, too. Anyway, I don't know why he's so damn stubborn, but he just is. It's like this one time when some homeless guy showed up at his store and sold him a picture of this crazy painting of sunflowers that didn't look nothing like sunflowers at all for two bucks. Mom and me kept telling him the painting wasn't worth anything 'cuz it wasn't even a real painting, but some souped-up poster like they sell at Woolworth's, but he wouldn't listen to us. He had his mind fixed that we'd lucked out somehow and gotten our hands on a lost masterpiece. So he had me get all these books from the library, and sure enough, the same picture was in this book of paintings by some guy named Vincent Van Gogh, who must have been one crazy motherfucker 'cuz the book said he cut off his own ear.

You should have seen how excited Dad was to see that picture in the book. He couldn't stop talking about it for two straight weeks. Then he came home one night with this fancy paper and wrapped the picture with it. The next day, he had me dress up all nice and go with him to this fancy art auction place in Manhattan called Christie's.

Boy, did I ever feel stupid explaining why we were there to the lady who met us at the door. She just stood there and listened all quietly until I was done translating for Dad. But then you should have seen the look on her face when Dad finally unwrapped the masterpiece and laid it on her.

Any other guy with even a tiny bit of pride woulda chucked that worthless picture in the trash after that. But not Dad. He insisted on bringing it back home like it was still valuable and the lady at Christie's was lying to him. It's still up in our living room. Even the bastards who robbed us knew better than to take that piece of shit.

Considering all that, I know there's no way I can get out of reading the letter. So I make like I'm reading it real carefully. Then I look up and say, "It says they'll put your name in a drawing if you buy magazines. But you didn't win any money yet."

"You sure?"

I nod. And I guess he finally believes me 'cuz he takes the letter from me and tries to smile like it's no big deal and he's not even a tiny bit disappointed. But he's never been cool at stuff like that, so even I can tell he's sad.

A part of me feels bad for the guy 'cuz I know about all the bad luck he's had starting from being born an orphan and not having the money to go to college even though he did real well on this big test they have in Korea and how he lost his store and all that 'cuz of his greedy Jew landlord and their team of greedy Jew lawyers. But on the other hand, is he really serious? Does he really think someone's just gonna hand him ten million dollars for doing nothing?

"Is that it?" I say.

He nods.

"Then we're gonna go."

He nods again.

But just as I turn around to get the hell outta there, he says, "Wait."

I turn back. He holds up two tokens and says, "Get something to eat for you and your brother. And, Minho. Don't worry about your Atari. I'll get you a new one soon. I promise."

I believe him completely. Why wouldn't I, considering that he couldn't even get me one the first time around and all he does is hang out with losers at the park all day waiting for someone to hand him ten million bucks for doing nothing?

Not that I'm optimistic or always see the good in people. But the one thing I got faith in is people. They always let you down somehow.

CHAPTER 8

THE SLICES AT Marino's ain't that bad, but they really suck 'cuz the guy who makes 'em, this hairy guy named Salami, is from Afghanistan, where all they ever cook is goats. But it's still the only place you can get a slice and a small Italian ice for a token, so the hell with pizzas made by real fucking guidos.

Me and Steven get our slices and sit at this table by the window. Across the street, there's some ugly mutt tied to the payphones outside the A&P, where the manager, this sick fuck named Mr. De Falco who has the worst fucking dragon breath you can ever imagine, used to pay me five bucks a week to sweep the sidewalk before I quit to do my paper route. The dog's ugly and mean and starts barking like crazy at the people walking by like it would bite their heads off in half a second if it weren't all tied up.

While we're looking at the ugly worthless mutt, Fatty goes and buys himself two slices, which he drowns with pepper, garlic, chili peppers, and powder cheese, basically everything on the counter, then kills in less than a minute. I gotta hand it to the guy. He can really put it away, which sort of explains why his parents gotta work so hard.

I guess the bastard's still hungry, though, 'cuz he starts pouring cheese right into his mouth straight from the bottle like it was soda.

"Hey, what d'you think you're doing!" yells Salami from behind the counter.

Fatty puts the cheese down and plays dumb.

"What? You kids think this stuff grows on trees? I gotta pay good money for that stuff," says Salami.

Fatty just shrugs, but grabs the cheese again as soon as the guy turns his back on him.

Of course, all that time, Africa just sits across from me staring at my pizza. He ain't exactly drooling, but it just ain't that fun to stuff your face in front of a guy who's got nothing to eat. So I offer him a bite, but he says no and just goes on sitting there.

What can I do? It's a free country. And it ain't like I can buy him a slice or like I didn't offer him some, right? And it ain't like Africa's broke. The kid's just super cheap like that. Like I've never seen the kid ever spring for a soda. It could be two hundred degrees out, and the kid could be dying of thirst, he'll just wait until he sees a water fountain or drink from some hydrant rather than spend 50 goddamn cents for a soda.

So I turn away from him and look out the window again. The mutt's still there, but it ain't barking no more 'cuz Roman's there, holding this bag of groceries and untying the dog. I guess the douchebag got himself a pet since we last saw him. Either that or he's real slick and just got himself one right now.

I don't know if Roman sees us, but he walks off down the street real quick without turning in our direction even once. For a moment, I think about going over to talk to him since he might have seen who ripped me off, but then I remind myself that the guy hates my guts so why the hell would he help me even if he could? If the tables were turned, and I was in Roman's shoes, I wouldn't help me, either. So the hell with it. Knowing what a fucking baby he is, the guy's probably waiting for me to apologize, but fuck him. So I messed up and did him wrong. That don't mean I gotta get on my knees and be all on the guy's dick. The Jewish landlord fucked over my dad. And you don't see that son of a bitch saying no I'm-sorry's. So fuck it. Roman can wait forever or until the super learns to speak English without no Goya accent, you ain't gonna catch me make no goddamn apology.

Just then, a crumpled napkin hits me in the head. I turn around, and Fatty says, "Yo, you think that nigger used food stamps even without Hindu Tim?"

He's trying to be funny about the time Roman tried to hide his food stamps. I guess the guy was embarrassed, even though all of us know him and his mom get food stamps and they got big blocks of government cheese in their fridge. Not that I blame the guy. Steven and me get free lunch at school, and we hate it, too, when they call the kids to the lunch line by full, reduced, and free lunch, so everyone can see who gets what.

"What the fuck happened between you and that nigger, anyway?" says Fatty. "How come you guys are like enemies now?"

"Nothing."

"Come on, bro. You can tell us. Did he try to feel you up or did he just ask to see your busted-up wee wee?"

"No, Fatty. He told me he has a crush on you. Says he's been dreaming about you since the first day he saw your big tits."

"Real funny, bro. Too bad I ain't no faggot."

I fling what's left of my pizza, half the crust, at him. It hits him on the forehead and bounces off onto the table.

"Yo, chill," he says. Then he picks up the crust and yanks his arm back. But instead of flinging it back at me, he just pops it in his mouth and says, "Thanks, bro. The crust's my favorite part."

I didn't mean to give him the crust. But the hell with it. If it'll shut him up for a little while, why the hell not?

But of course nothing can shut Fatty up for long, so he starts yapping again and says, "But really, bro. What happened with you and that nigger?"

"Nothing, Fatty. Will you shut the fuck up already?"

I guess you don't have to be no genius to figure out that that ain't true. But I ain't really proud of what I did. So Fatty can ask me a hundred times. I ain't gonna tell him shit. With the mouth Fatty's got, telling him's like telling the whole world. It's 'cuz of him that everyone knows about me getting that operation and dickheads call me "Stitch" behind my back. So you can bet your life I ain't gonna make that mistake twice.

Fatty grabs the bottle of powdered cheese again and starts drinking it down. This time, though, Salami comes over and yanks the bottle out of his hand.

"That's it. Get out. Get out of my pizzeria!"

"Goddamn, Salami. You're fucking cheap," says Fatty.

"You watch your mouth. And get the hell out."

"Fine, bro. Just don't touch me, all right, you goddamn fucking Hindu."

"How many times I have to tell you? I am not from India!"

"Yeah, yeah. That's what they all say."

We all get up and go. Not that getting kicked out of some crummy pizzeria makes you feel real hot or anything. But it ain't no big deal 'cuz we're done eating and we know Salami ain't picking on us. The guy's a dick to everyone.

CHAPTER 9

I DON'T REMEMBER which one of us thought up the phone gag, but it's always good for a couple of laughs, which is exactly what you need when you keep thinking about the Atari you don't have no more.

Not that I'm whining 'cuz like I told you before, I hate whiners more than I hate spics and chinks and ajussies and Afghanistan pizza guys. But getting your stuff ripped off while you're stuck at some crummy church picnic you didn't even wanna go to in the first place really sucks, especially when the picnic's a hundred corny Korean people eating kimchi and singing "Kumbayah."

Not that I got anything against church. I know plenty of people who believe that shit. But I just don't wanna sit there on Sundays and waste my time listening to bullshit. Take my Atari, for instance. I can go see a pastor. I can go to church every day and pray to God for months. But ain't none of my stuff ever gonna come back to me 'cuz of Jesus or the Holy Ghost.

It ain't even that all the stuff that got stolen was super valuable or that I can't live without them. It ain't like that at all. The TV they took was this crappy old Zenith that Dad bought for twenty bucks off of the same bum who sold him the Van Gogh. And my comics weren't worth much, even though I went around talking them up all the time and a couple of them were number ones and twos, 'cuz none of them were in mint condition.

As for my Atari, even though I always went on and on about how great the games were, except for Defender and Missile Command, where you can do this trick to get the letters *"RF"* to come up on the bottom of the screen by firing all your missiles on the thirteenth screen, the rest of my 42 games were garbage, especially Joust and E.T., which were complete rip-offs and no ways worth the money I had to shell out for them.

That's what really gets me. If you haven't figured it out by now, I ain't no little rich kid whose parents get him whatever he wants whenever he snaps his fingers. I don't even get an allowance. So you can just imagine what I had to do to get all those games.

Now, I'm not saying I have it as bad as the kids in Ethiopia who ain't got nothing to eat so their stomachs stick out from some weird disease and have flies camped out in their eyes and nostrils, but doing a paper route in Elmhurst ain't much better. First of all, you gotta wake up at five in the morning, when it's still pitch black out and everybody you see looks like some mugger. Then you gotta go in and out of all these crummy buildings, where all the bulbs are busted so you can't see a damn thing. But the absolute worst part is having to go around at the end of every week to try to collect money from the deadbeats you delivered to all week.

Don't get me wrong. I know there are some really nice, honest people out there who get their paper and pay for it on time the way they're supposed to, but my customers were all cheap fucking assholes who pretended not to be home even though I could hear them through the door just so they could stiff a little kid out of three bucks. The only time the money was even close to decent was during Christmas, when people give you an extra dollar for tip 'cuz they feel sorry for you. So if you're crazy or desperate and thinking of doing a paper route, start right before Christmas, then quit right after New Year's. But then if all that's true, why the hell did I do the paper route for two fucking years?

Easy. Because I wanted to make sure I learned self-discipline and the value of hard work 'cuz those are the building blocks that will prepare me for success in the future.

What a crock of shit!

Like I give a crap about self-discipline and hard work. I may be just a kid, but even I know that the only thing anyone who goes on and on about those things—gym teachers and tae kwon do guys mostly—really wants is to make your life just as shitty and miserable as their own.

The real reason I stuck with the paper route for two years was that as bad as it was, it still paid way better than all the other shitty jobs I had before: selling Christmas cards door-to-door—yeah, I called the number on the back of the comic book—sweeping the sidewalk outside the A&P, shoveling snow, and folding the Sunday paper at the Optimo.

So being a slave for the *Daily News* was the only way I could make sure I wasn't the only kid on the block without an Atari. Trust me. I've been the only kid on the block without a lot of things lots of times, and it sucks. Which is why, if I had it to do all over, I'd do the paper route again in a second. But that ain't an option no more 'cuz Mr. Arabian, the dickhead who runs the routes in my neighborhood, fired my ass 'cuz of Mrs. Trevite, this crazy old white lady who was the worst customer I ever had.

It all started with Mrs. Trevite deducting money from what she owed me for all the papers she said she didn't get. Usually I'm good at getting even super cheap people like that to pay the full amount, but she had this piece of paper with all the dates written down when there was no paper outside her door. The only thing was, I had delivered the paper to her on those days. But there are some arguments you just can't win, especially when the person you're arguing is some super crazy old bitch.

Anyway, I figured some neighbor of hers was swiping the papers off her, which is what happens most of the time. So I hid in the stairwell one day to see who was taking 'em. And wouldn't you know it. It was the old lady. She grabbed 'em herself and was making a big stink about not getting the paper just so she could stiff me. So when she brought out her list at the end of that week, I called her a fucking liar and just stopped delivering to her. I figured that was the end of that. I had no idea she'd call up the paper and complain to Mr. Arabian's boss about how I was a fresh-mouthed punk with no respect who'd threatened her and how dare they hire thugs like me and all that. I tried to explain what really happened to Mr. Arabian. But that's the thing with grown-ups. When it's just your word against a grown-up's, grown-ups will always take the grown-up's side. It's like some dickhead code where dickheads gotta stick together.

That's partly why doing the phone gag cheers me up so much. What we do is, we pick up the two phones next to each other and dial the operator. When they come on, we ask each of them how much they charge for a blowjob. Then we put the two phones together but with one phone turned upside down, so the earpiece goes next to the mouthpiece, and the two operators end up yelling at each other for a while.

Sure, it ain't the funniest gag in the world and it ain't very mature, but I never said I was mature, did I? What matters is we thought it up and it's still something to do, which is better than sitting at home waiting for the Pixx guy to call.

Anyway, after we do the phone gag a half dozen times, this ice cream truck pulls up at the corner and all we can hear is the damn ice cream song: *"Dun-da-dun-da-dun-da-da. Dun-da. Dun-da. Da-da."*

A second later, a dozen little kids pop out of nowhere and start running toward it like they would just die if they didn't get a damn popsicle.

I don't know who made up the ice cream song, but the guy deserves 10 raises 'cuz the music goes right inside your head and makes you want an ice cream so bad. So even though I wasn't even thinking about a popsicle a second ago, my mouth suddenly fills up with all this spit and all I can think of is how am I gonna get me an ice cream.

I dig through my pockets, but all I got is a couple of nickels, not enough for even a lousy twin pop, which is the fucking Holland of popsicles.

So I turn to Fatty to ask him for some money, but he's on to me and says, "I ain't got no money, bro. I was about to ask you."

It's what he always says, and it's the biggest goddamn lie. I don't know what kind of allowance he gets or if he just steals from his parents all the time, but the bastard somehow always has money.

So I say, "Come on, Fatty. Don't be like that."

"Like what? I'd lend you if I had, bro. I swear. I'll get money later from Jin. But I'm broke. You can even check my pockets," he says, patting the front of his shorts for show.

"I ain't gonna dig through your damn pockets, Fatty."

"I told you, bro. I ain't got."

"Goddamn, Fatty. You and me been friends since we were little. And you know that if I had a quarter I'd lend it to you in a second.

But if you're too cheap to spot me a lousy quarter, then the hell with you!"

He shakes his head, then says, like he's all pissed off or something, "Calm the fuck down, bro. You want a fucking twin pop that bad, I'll get you one. Shit! All this fucking bullshit for a fucking twin pop!"

CHAPTER 10

NOT THAT ANY of our moms is a looker or anything. They're all ajoomas, so even if they go to hair salons a lot like Fatty and Africa's moms do, none of 'em looks anything close to Roman's mom, who's real fine and all super sexy even though she's black 'cuz she was just 15 when she had Roman, which, by the way, is why, whenever we used to go anywhere with Roman and his mom, all these horny guys would come up to her and try to hit on her. And not just black guys, neither. White guys, Spanish guys, everybody, even some Chinese guys.

Roman wouldn't ever say nothing, but every time it happened, you could tell he was fucking pissed 'cuz he'd get all quiet like he was off in his own world thinking up ways to blow the scumbags away. I'd be pissed, too, it it was my mom and she flirted back all the time. I'm not saying she's a slut or anything, but I swear to God, she can get you hard just by saying "Hello."

Anyway, even with all that with our own moms, the ajooma behind the counter at V&B's something else. She's got this face that looks like a rusted tin can. It's something you'd put up on your window on Halloween to scare away ghosts.

As soon as we walk in the store, Ms. Can Face puts down the newspaper she's been reading and looks up at us like she's got us all figured out and we better not try nothing stupid.

I guess she's had tons of kids try to steal from her 'cuz she keeps her eyes glued on us the whole time and doesn't even play it off like she's asking us if we need help like some storeowners do. It's exactly what I'd do, too, if I was her and a bunch of no-good kids came strolling inside my store.

Not that it makes any difference, though, 'cuz Fatty does this slick move where he goes to the freezer and holds up a toasted almond bar with one hand, asks her the price, and jams four twin pops inside his shorts with the other hand all at the same time.

The ajooma's eyes are wide open and she's looking right at him, but she doesn't see nothing. It's like Fatty's Obi-Wan, doing some Jedi mind trick.

Then, as we file back out, the ajooma leans over the counter and says, "Wait a minute, boys."

Right away, I get this feeling like we're about to get busted and get all set to bolt out of there. Not that I'm fast or anything, but I know I can outrun some old ajooma any day even if I've got a hard-on. That's another weird thing about me. Lots of things will get me hard, but doing anything bad will get me hard so quick, it ain't even funny.

The only thing is, she doesn't tell us to freeze or empty our pockets. Instead, she just says, "Here, take this."

She then hands each of us pamphlets for some stupid church retreat, with pictures of all these goody-goodys holding hands with tears coming down their faces.

"Listen to your parents and go to church, boys," she says.

Fatty puts the pamphlet in his pocket, then smiles his goody-goody smile and says, in perfect Korean, without sounding even the tiniest bit sarcastic, "Don't worry, ma'am. We've all been saved, and we're all going to heaven."

You gotta hand it to the kid. His goody-goody act's so good, you gotta wonder if he practices at home or something. He bows at all the right times and his Korean's perfect, even though he was born right here in Elmhurst Hospital. I guess it's all a good thing. Otherwise, he'd get busted all the time 'cuz he's the biggest klepto I know.

One time, when we were kids, he swiped enough stuff from the A&P for all of us to pig out at the railroad tracks: five frozen TV dinners, two boxes of Italian ice, a pack of hot dogs, two two-liter bottles of Mountain Dew, and half a watermelon. How the hell he walked out with all that stuff right past six cashiers, none of us will ever know.

Anyway, once we're outside the V&B, we walk down the block real cool like we didn't just swipe nothing from nowhere, then turn the corner and sit down on some stoop, right in front of this corny sign that says, *"No Loitering. Forget the dog and beware of the owner."*

Talk about a stupid sign. It's cornier than the one they got at swimming pools that says, *"Welcome to our ool."* They might as well put up a sign that says, *"I'm a dick, so please take a dump on my stoop."*

Fatty takes the twin pops out, hands 'em to us, and says, "Enjoy 'em, fellers."

Sure, it's kind of nasty that Fatty had 'em in his shorts all that time. But at least they got wrappers on 'em and we didn't have to pay jack.

Fatty kills his in three bites. It takes me and Africa a little longer. Steven, on the other hand, takes forever and sort of half nibbles at his like he's trying to make it last all morning or something. It's how he is with everything, super slow like a little baby. Who knows when the hell the kid will ever grow up.

Anyway, when I'm done with mine and about to fling the popsicle stick into the street so that a wino will have enough supplies to build himself an arts-and-crafts basket, a tard car pulls up right in front of us.

The door swings open and some kid in a wheelchair gets lifted out. While that's going on, a bunch of retards with thick glasses and drool running down their chins stare out at us through the windows with these dumb looks on their faces. They're too stupid even for special ed and have to go to a special school where they teach you how to eat with a spoon and drink out of a straw. Still, they're smart enough to give us the finger. So we give the finger right back, then look for something to throw at 'em. If it were Halloween, we'd bomb the shit out of their bus with eggs. But it's summer and all we got to throw is a couple of crushed soda cans from the garbage, but even that's better than nothing.

The driver doesn't even bother to say shit to us after the cans hit the window, which's a good thing 'cuz we'd just run and he's got way better things to do, like scrape drool and boogers off the windows. Anyway, it ain't like we're hitching a ride on the bumpers or nothing or he even gives a damn about the retards on his bus, so what the hell does he care, right?

When the tard car finally pulls away, Fatty says, "Holy shit. That's her, man! That's the girl who'll do you-know-what for five bucks."

I look up and see this girl on the other side of the street who looks kind of Filipino or Thai. Whatever she is, she ain't a bad-looking LBFM. I mean, she ain't super sexy like Hindu Tim's sister, who always looks like she's about to go fuck some guy's brains out, but she's definitely no flat-chested dog like some of the girls at school.

Fatty whips out the Binaca he's always carrying around and zaps himself in the mouth. Then he cups his hands around his mouth and shouts, "What's up, honey? Wanna know where the beef is at?"

There's no way in hell she couldn't have heard him. Still, she just plays it off like we're not even there and she's got a hundred better things to do than waste her time with us.

But it takes more than that to stop Fatty. He takes out his marker, holds it out in front of his crotch, and starts humping the air. Then the horny bastard shouts, "I can rock your world, girl!"

Most girls would blush, giggle, or curse us out after something like that, but she doesn't say nothing. The snooty bitch just walks away like we're scum and she'd never waste two seconds of her precious time on us.

Of course, none of that bothers Fatty at all. He just turns to the rest of us with this huge grin on his face and says, "Did you see how that girl was looking at me? I'm telling you, bro. She wants to get with me."

"Give me a break, Fatty. No one's that desperate," I say.

"Don't be jealous, bro. You'll see. I'm gonna finger-pop that girl before the week's over. Then I'll have her wrapped around my dick."

"Keep dreaming."

"I ain't gotta dream about nothing. Remember, unlike you two faggots, I've done it for real."

"Your little sister don't count, Fatty. Neither does your right hand, or your left."

"Real funny. Too bad it ain't true. Shit, I haven't been a virgin since I was nine years old. How do you think I became bow-legged? I wasn't born like this, you know."

"Right, I forgot. You did it with that phantom girlfriend of yours in Korea."

"Trust me, Pete. She wasn't no phantom. No phantom's got tits like hers. You should have seen 'em, bro. They were huge. Most Korean girls got tits the size of nickels. This girl had tits the size of watermelons. Goddamn! Just thinking about them's getting me hard."

"Man, you're full of shit."

"I'll say it again, bro. You can believe me or not. That's up to you. But all I'm gonna say is, don't hate me just 'cuz I got some and you haven't. It ain't my fault that your thing's all messed up. Blame that welfare doctor, bro. All I know is, it ain't like I even tried that hard. I mean, all I had to do was give her my Walkman. What can I say, bro? Girls are just on my dick for some reason."

"Name one."

"One what?"

"One girl who's on your dick."

"I just told you."

"Besides that girl from Korea. Someone who wasn't blind and retarded."

"Forget this, bro. I ain't gotta prove nothing to you homos."

"Come on, Fatty. I dare you."

"Yeah, Fatty. Come on," says Africa, joining in.

"Fine, you bowl-headed motherfucker," he says to Africa. "You want names, I'll give you names."

Then, Fatty leans in real close to us and says real soft, like he's letting us in on some secret, "You know Hindu Tim's sister, right?"

Africa and me look at each other like Fatty's crazy.

Then I say, "Get outta here, Fatty. Hindu Tim's sister's like 18 years old. Why the hell would she do it with some fat little kid for?"

"How the hell do I know? Maybe she heard about me or maybe she was just super horny. All I know is I went over to that sucker's house last week to see if I could get some games off him. I think it was Thursday or Friday. Anyway, he wasn't there, but his sister told me to come inside for a while. So I go in there, and she starts asking me all these questions. You know, stupid shit, like if I got a girlfriend and shit like that. And I play it cool and say no. Then she asks me if I'm a virgin. So I tell her yes, even though it ain't true, 'cuz I know how older girls like to think they're teaching you shit. Then she says her back hurts and could I please rub some lotion on it. I say sure. So I start massaging her back. Of course, I have the craziest hard-on the whole time 'cuz she's fucking hot, you know. And then she starts making these moaning sounds. And then I just kind of lost it. So I pull it out right there and say, 'Baby, it's now your turn to give me a massage.'"

"Bullshit," I say.

But Fatty doesn't even bat an eye. He just goes on with his story. "The next thing you know, she's all over me and giving me this handjob right there on her couch. Up and down. Up and down. I swear to God. It was like one of those letters in the magazines. Shit, that's what I should do, bro. I should write a fucking letter. Maybe they'll even print it and shit."

"You're full of shit, Fatty," I say.

"I swear it's true. You can even go ask her right now if you don't believe me. What am I gonna lie about this for?"

"How the hell do I know? But I know you're lying 'cuz if it was true, there's no way in hell you woulda been able to keep your mouth shut all this time."

"That don't mean shit, bro. I didn't tell you 'cuz she made me promise not to tell. But what can I say? You guys forced it out of me. Honestly, it feels kind of good to get it off my chest. You know, like a weight's been lifted off me. I guess it's like what it says in the Bible, the truth shall set you free."

Africa and me just look at each other and shake our heads. It's like everything that comes out of Fatty's mouth is total bullshit. But then again, what are you gonna do, right? Like sometimes, even bullshit's better than nothing, right?

Take myself, for instance. The only thing even remotely sexy that ever happened to me besides watching pornos at Roman's house with his mom, which she let us do 'cuz she said they were educational, was Linda Rojas letting me feel up her tits at her birthday party a month before she moved away to Staten Island. Not that it was a big deal or anything 'cuz she was pretty much the school slut and let all the boys at the party do that. Still, for a

12-year-old girl, she had these massive tits you wouldn't believe, which just makes you wonder what she's going to look like when she gets older.

Who knows? Maybe if she hadn't moved away, I might have gotten laid already or at least gotten even a crummy handjob. Instead, I'm walking around all the time with a hard-on, crank-calling the operator, and jerking off every chance I get.

"Yo, you guys ready for another treat?" says Fatty, again with his moron grin.

I'm not sure what he's talking about. Neither does Africa or Steven. But before we can figure out what, a hand shoots out of nowhere and yanks me up off the stoop by my ear.

I yell 'cuz it hurts like hell. Then I see some crazy-looking ajussy wearing a Marlboro hat, standing there with my ear in one hand and Fatty's ear in the other.

At first, I think maybe it's some guy from the building. Some dickheads can get real pissed if you sit on their stoop or on their car like you're contaminating it or something. Like this one time, this guy from around the corner from the Leben Home made a big stink about us hanging out on his stoop and went off on us like some tough guy about how everyone's gotta respect private property otherwise the whole world will turn into a zoo. That's the thing I love about tough guys. All they're ever really doing is bullying you into doing something, but they always gotta make it seem like they're persuading you somehow. What a load of shit! I'd like to see what kind of speech the guy would've made if we'd been big black guys and not just little Chinese kids.

Anyway, I'm waiting for the dipshit to make the same speech, when the guy opens his mouth and says, in perfect ajussy English, "You little thief. You stole from my store."

The first thing that pops into my head is, so this is the lucky bastard who gets to see the beauty queen at the V&B butt naked every night. No wonder the guy looks so pissed off.

The second thing is, yelling solves nothing when some dumb fuck's upset and screaming at you 'cuz you swiped what's basically a couple of quarters from him. So I take a deep breath and calmly explain to the guy how we're orphans with no parents and no money and the only reason we made off with those twin pops is 'cuz we haven't had a real meal in three weeks and I can't see at night because of malnutrition.

Yeah, right!

Like the guy cares about anything except how many nectarines to sell for a dollar.

So I just say, "I didn't steal nothing," which's the truth 'cuz Fatty's the one who stole the twin pops, not me.

"You lying. You little thief, all of you, stealing ice cream and magazine my store!"

"We didn't steal nothing!"

"You dare continuing lying? You no have no shame? Where your mother? Where your father? I teach you lesson you never forget."

The guy sounds just like Benny Hill when he dresses up as a Chinese guy and says, "Not nece celery. Solly, we no have no fly lice."

But now ain't exactly the time to tell him that. And anyway, the guy's probably never heard of Benny Hill. So I just say, "I told you. We didn't steal nothing. So get off me before we call the cops for child abuse!"

I know I'm reaching at straws, but I've gotten out of lots of situations like that 'cuz a lot of ajussies get real scared any time you bring up cops. But I guess the word's out on the ajussy network 'cuz our new best friend doesn't buy it. He just yanks our ears even harder and starts dragging us up the street.

The whole thing's fucking embarrassing 'cuz it's like the guy knows some secret Tiger Chung Lee pressure point and it don't do us no good to try to punch and kick the bastard.

All I can do is look over at Africa and Steven, who look like they're in shock. Who knows what the hell Tiger Chung Lee's gonna do to us?

From the look on Fatty's face, I know he's thinking the same thing. The last time he got caught stealing, the Hindu at the Optimo took him to the back and roughed him up 'til there were red handmarks all over his face. Sure we threw a bag of burning dog shit in his store the next day, but as funny as that shit was, I'd rather not go through that again if I can help it.

CHAPTER 11

I KNOW IT'S weird, but I actually ask myself, what would B.J. do if he were in my situation? Not that B.J. would ever let himself get in a dumbass situation like us. There's no way in hell he'd ever let no loser ajussy push him around or let anyone rip him off.

That's the thing with Jin's brother. Even if you hated his guts, which a lot of people did 'cuz he could be a real dick sometimes and mess with you and make you feel like shit for no reason, you still had to hand it to the guy for having balls. I mean, he wasn't much bigger than me or Fatty, but he'd fight anyone anywhere if they so much as looked at him wrong.

I totally understand why the Goblins let him be in their gang even though he's Korean and they're Chinese. Not that I wanna be in some gang with a bunch of chinks or anything. Like I told you before, I hate chinks even more than I hate spics. So if I ever join a real gang, you better believe it's gonna be some gang like KP, which's the only gang out there worth joining. They don't let no chinks or spics in that gang and only rob people who ain't Korean, kind of like Robin Hood but in modern times.

Don't get me wrong. Even though I may go on and on sometimes about gangs, being in a gang ain't my dream or nothing. I know most gangsters are brainless dickheads who couldn't count to 20, and the only reason they're in a gang in the first place is 'cuz they're fucking cowards who couldn't do a goddamn thing on their own. But then again, I guess there definitely are some perks to being in a gang. Hell, it beats working at some crummy fish store like Fatty's dad or fixing shoes like my dad used to do. And at least people would be scared of you, you'd have money, and you'd have all these slutty girls hanging around you all the time. I mean, you should have seen how all these girls practically threw themselves at B.J. all the time.

Not that I think every kid in a gang gets girls like that. I ain't stupid. I know for every B.J. out there, there's a ton of ugly zit-faced thugs who couldn't pay girls to go around with them. Which is why you gotta give B.J. credit, though it probably helps that he's one of those goddamn handsome guys who still manage to look all tough somehow. Him and Jin both look like that, which just makes you sick to your stomach sometimes 'cuz it just doesn't seem fair. Like how come there are kids who look like them, then there are kids like Fatty, whose faces look like a lump of old pizza dough?

I don't mean to go on and on about B.J., but the guy was genuinely cool. Like he could treat you like shit for months and get all mad and make like he was about to kick your ass, but then it'd turn out that he was just bluffing to see whether you had guts or not. And as long as you proved you had guts, he'd turn around and joke with you in this way that made you feel all cool, too. For instance, he'd look you right in the eye and say, "Just let me know when you kids wanna lose it 'cuz I know a place. And your first time's always better with a pro."

I mean, how cool is that? I know a lot of kids can't wait to grow up, so they can be astronauts or firefighters or some other corny shit like that. But if you ask me, a lot of the reason why I can't wait to get older is so that I can say stuff like that. "Just let me know when you kids wanna lose it 'cuz I know a place. And your first time's always better with a pro."

Of course, none of us had the guts to take him up on it. But I sometimes wish I had. That way, at least I wouldn't still be a goddamn virgin who's walking around with a hard-on half the day. Take now, for instance.

I swear to God it's true. The fucking ajussy from the V&B, whose breath smells like a fucking ashtray, is dragging me and Fatty by our fucking ears, and all I can think about is how humongous and soft Linda Rojas's tits were. I don't know which lucky bastard out in Staten Island's feeling them up right now, but I'd bet just about anything that the dumb fuck doesn't know how good he has it.

Anyway, we're halfway back to the V&B and all these people on the street are staring at us, when I finally think to blurt out, "But Kato's in the stairs."

"What?" The ajussy stops and looks at me with this confused expression on his face.

"Kato. We forgot Kato. Kato's in the stairs."

"What? Who Kato? Who in what stair?"

Instead of an answer, I kick him hard right in his shin.

He lets out a yelp, then lets go of our ears for a split second, which is all we need to start booking down the street.

Even Steven, who can't run that good 'cuz of asthma, keeps up with us somehow. Thank God. 'Cuz it would suck if we ever got caught 'cuz of him.

Behind us, the ajussy starts shouting curses in Korean like he can't believe he just fell for the oldest trick in the book.

Who the fuck is Kato?

How the hell do I know? If you wanna know so bad, go ask the fucking Green Hornet.

What I do know is that knowing how ajussies are, the fucking asshole will probably go back and tell his dog-faced wife some bullshit story about how it's a good thing he learned tae kwon do back in the day 'cuz two dozen no-good street thugs pulled machetes on him and he barely escaped with his life.

The fucking bastard. I hope some other ajussy opens up a store right across the street from him and puts him out of business. Either that or his cheap Jew landlord will kick his ass out to the curb the way they did my dad.

CHAPTER 12

FATTY'S BENT OVER with his hands on his knees like he's about to heave the ramen and two slices he had for breakfast. But he doesn't. Thank God. 'Cuz that would be nasty.

Instead, he spits a loogy, then wipes the sweat off his face on the front of his shirt. The bastard's soaking wet. And he's got two huge sweat rings under his pits, which means we're in for a treat 'cuz he's got worse b.o. than Hindu Tim.

Fatty then turns to me and says, "I'm telling you, bro. We gotta stop running so much and start fighting. We ain't gonna get no respect if all we do is run from everybody."

The bastard makes it sound so damn easy. But he's always the first one to run, so what the fuck is he talking about?

But I don't say nothing and just make like I'm not winded, which ain't easy 'cuz all there is to breathe is hot air that feels like it's coming right out of a fucking hair dryer. It's almost like we're in some desert except instead of sand, there's just garbage and flies.

Up ahead, the loonie brigade's out in full force walking in circles outside the Leben Home. Half of them are in their pajamas. The other half's in thick winter coats and wool caps like it's the middle of January. Every single one of them's smoking butts they bummed off people or picked up off the street, and muttering to themselves as they wave their hands in front of them. That's the thing with crazy people. They always move their hands a lot.

Mr. Schnell, this crazy old guy who lives in the apartment next to us, told me once that the loonies are supposed to be supervised at all times by the city, but I've never seen anyone following them around. Either the city ain't doing its job or the bozos doing the supervising are camouflaged and look just as crazy as all the rest of them.

From behind me, Africa comes over, dragging Steven by the hand, and says, "Pete, I think something's wrong with your brother."

I wipe the sweat off my forehead on my arm and look over at the kid, who hasn't said a word since Fatty stepped in shit outside the car wash.

His face's the same color as chalk and he starts hacking like some old bum who's about to keel over. Then he looks up at me, and there's blood oozing out the side of his mouth like in all those old movies. Mom and Dad have taken him to a half dozen doctors, but they all say the same thing. There's nothing they can do for him, and he's got exactly six months to live.

Wise up!

Truth is, the kid's got a little asthma from all the fucking roach eggs we're breathing in all the time. That's another thing I forgot to tell you. The Holland looks like an apartment building, but it's really a roach farm, where all these tough roaches fight it out to see who's the meanest. They don't bug me that much 'cuz I'm sort of used to them, but it drives Mom crazy. Every six months, she tries to get them with roach bombs. You should see how our apartment looks afterwards. It's like *The Day After*—which wasn't scary at all even though all the teachers made such a big fucking deal about it, which just goes to show you what fucking chickens they are—except instead of dead people, there's hundreds of dead roaches.

"You want your inhaler?" I say to the kid.

He nods. So I take it out and hand it to him. That's mostly what I'm supposed to do for the kid when he gets sick, make sure he gets his inhaler.

Anyway, watching him suck on the little piece of plastic, I can't help but feel sorry for the kid 'cuz he's gotta be the sickliest kid on the planet. Besides having asthma and being born premature, the kid's got a dozen allergies, which is why we had to throw his cat away in the railroad tracks and why he always wants to go down there all the time. Before you get all huffy and say how could we do something like that to a poor cat, let me just say that we tried for a month to find it a good home. But no one wanted it. Fatty said he'd take the cat, but brought it back two days later 'cuz his mom wouldn't let him keep it no more 'cuz it was scratching up their couch. The same with Jin and Africa.

If you ask me, we should have never got it in the first place. But I guess Mom wanted to try to cheer Steven up with it on account of how he ain't got no friends. And it worked for a while, too. The kid spent hours playing with the cat and wouldn't go nowhere without it. I swear to God, it seemed like the kid liked that stupid cat more than anything else, which just made it that much harder to get rid of it.

I guess we could have taken it back to the animal shelter out on Long Island, where we got it from. But then Steven made this huge fuss where he just cried and cried 'cuz he was sure they would kill it. Mom tried to explain to him how that would only happen after 30 days, but you can't really reason with a kid who's just bawling all the time.

So Mom and me decided it'd be better to just put the cat down by the railroad tracks, where it'd have a better chance of making it since there's so many damn rats down there for it to munch on. But I don't know what happened to the fucking cat. I don't know if someone found it and took it home or if Fatty shot it with his BB gun—the fatass swears he didn't, but who knows?—or if it got run over by the train or turned wild and is roaming the bushes, hiding out from people. All I know is, we haven't seen it since, and I just hope it doesn't ever turn up dead and rotting somewhere 'cuz Steven would freak out like crazy if that ever happened.

Who knows how much weirder he'd get then? Maybe the kid would start yapping all the time like Fatty and go on and on about all the big black guys he beat up.

All kidding aside, I really worry about the kid sometimes 'cuz I don't know how he's ever gonna make it. It's all right now since he's only in the third grade, but what the hell's he gonna do when he gets to junior high and a whole gang of black kids comes up to him in the hallway and tells him to clean their sneakers with his tongue? You figure most kids would know better and start fighting back when something like that happens, but then again, there are tons of kids who'll start licking. So who the hell knows?

"What's wrong with him, bro?" says Fatty, sticking his fat head right over the kid and sucking up all the air.

"Nothing's wrong with him. He just has asthma," I say, wondering why Fatty has to be so damn nosy all of a sudden. It's not even like he gives a damn. He's always telling me to ditch the kid. Now, all of a sudden, he acts like he's the kid's best friend.

"You sure you don't have to take him to the hospital, bro? I saw this thing on TV about how this little kid your brother's age died from an asthma attack. The kid's throat closed up on him so tight he couldn't breathe. He died in the ambulance on the way to the hospital."

"You can't die from asthma, Fatty."

"Sure you can. It happens all the time. I told you, I saw it on TV. They even wrote an article about it in the *New York Times*."

That's the thing with Fatty. I'd bet anything that the kid's never even opened a copy of the *New York Times* in his whole life, but he'll go on and on about how he's read all sorts of crazy things in it like he reads that paper every day or something. The bastard will even tell you to call them to find out for sure. But I ain't in no mood to argue with the fucking dipshit. It ain't even like you can ever win an argument with him, anyway. Once, me and him argued for three weeks 'cuz he somehow got it into his head that Bruce Lee was really Korean and not Chinese and went on and on about how he could prove it 'cuz Bruce Lee's nose was shaped like a Korean's.

Bottom line is, arguing with Fatty just ain't worth it. So I turn back to Steven and say, "You all right?"

The kid just smiles this weak half smile, which brings out his dimples. And I kind of get it why girls are always making such a big deal about how cute he is. The kid does look just like a god-damn girl. Now, some people might think that's a good thing, but I don't. 'Cuz all that does is make kids think you're soft, which is the last thing Steven needs. As things are, he's got it bad enough. It's like, I can teach the kid to fight. And I can teach him to curse and tell him a thousand times to wise up. But I just know there ain't no way in hell that he's ever gonna get tough. And my parents ain't helping any neither by treating him like such a baby. For instance, they're always saying how he's weaker than other kids right in front of him. How the hell's a kid supposed to grow up tough when his own parents are telling him he's weak?

Anyway, Fatty opens his damn mouth again and says, "Damn, that was a close one. For a while there, I thought your brother was gonna bite it just like that kid on TV."

"Will you shut up already, Fatty," I say right up in his face.

"Why you gotta get all up in my face for, bro?" he says, like he actually doesn't have a clue that he's been bugging me the whole morning.

"You wanna know why? 'Cuz you're a fucking idiot! That's why!"

Fatty shakes his head. "I'm just telling you right now, bro. You keep messing with me and you're gonna regret it. 'Cuz I'm patient. But I ain't that patient."

"I'm real scared, Fatty."

"Just keep it up, bro." He then says, just like on the TV show, "You don't wanna see me get angry. You wouldn't like me when I'm angry."

He starts laughing. And I roll my eyes, wondering why I even bother trying to talk to the fat fuck sometimes.

So I go off and and sit with Steven on some parked car. A little later—while me and Steven are sitting there, staring across the street at this crazy old lady who's wearing a fake fur coat and who's got a cigar in one hand that's so burnt up that it's burning her finger—Fatty goes and smacks Africa on the head for no reason. It's almost like watching *The Three Stooges*, except with a fat kid and a skinny kid instead of three weird-looking white guys.

"What'd you hit me for?" says Africa.

"Shut the fuck up and fight," says Fatty, putting up his hands to slap-box.

"Leave me alone."

"What? You scared? Come on, bro. It'll do you good. Shit, if you'da slap-boxed with me more, you wouldn't have turned all chickenshit with Diego back at the park."

"Fuck you."

"You know it's true."

Africa doesn't say nothing.

Fatty goes to hit him again, but Africa smacks his hand away.

"That's more like it," says Fatty. "Come on. Let's do this."

"I said leave me alone."

"Come on, Africa. I know you're scared. But let's see you try to take me. Come on, bro. I'll fight you with one hand."

"Fuck off, Fatty."

"Don't tell me to fuck off. I backed you up against Diego. So don't tell me to fuck off."

"You didn't do shit. It was all Pete."

"It wasn't all Pete. I was all set to jump in and kick Diego's ass. Pete just beat me to it. That's all."

"Yeah, right."

"What? You calling me a liar?"

"Leave him alone, Fatty," I say. I swear, sometimes it feels like I'm babysitting three kids instead of one.

"This kid's fucked up, bro. We should kick him out of the Warriors like we did Roman."

"Will you leave Africa alone already?"

"What are you getting mad at me for, bro? I'm not the one who backed down to Diego. What's the point of him being down with the Warriors if he's gonna be a pussy all the time? How the hell do we know that he's not gonna wuss out on us again?"

"He ain't gonna wuss out on us."

"How do you know?"

"Fine, Fatty. You wanna be like that? How do we know you're not gonna wuss out on us later?"

"'Cuz I ain't no pussy."

"Neither's Africa. So leave him alone already. Goddamn! I swear, Fatty. You're like a little kid."

"Peter!" a scratchy old voice calls me from across the street.

I look over and see Mr. Schnell, waving from the other side of the street outside the Chinese sewing factory, where they put oranges out on the street for Chinese New Year.

"Yo, it's your best friend, bro," says Fatty, trying to be a comedian, as usual. "Go ask him if he saw who stole your shit. Maybe he'll feel sorry for you and give you a penny."

Not that I got anything against making penny-pinching-Jew jokes, but I flip Fatty the bird anyway 'cuz he's so damn corny. He's been telling that same joke for over a year now.

I start walking across the street. And Mr. Schnell, who sort of looks like a cross between Mayor Koch and Grampa from *The Munsters*, smiles at me. The guy's real crazy like all the other old white guys we know. Take his clothes, for instance. He wears the same old brown suit and bow tie every day and he goes around pushing this shopping cart, even though I've never seen the old guy actually lug anything in it. He just always has it with him for some reason.

As I get closer to the old guy, his smile disappears, I guess 'cuz he sees the bruise above my eye. It's still a little numb, which probably means it's gonna get even bigger by the time I go home tonight and Mom starts grilling me.

Still, for a moment, I half expect Mr. Schnell to say something funny like, "How's the other guy?" But he says pretty much the same as what Dad said, then starts nagging me something awful.

"You're a good boy, Peter. But fighting in the street is for hooligans. If you want to learn to fight for real, go to the boxing gym. There, you will be tested like a man."

I look down at my feet. It ain't that I'm ashamed or nothing, but the old guy just has this way of making you feel not so hot. Not that I think he's right. I've been to a boxing gym. It was at some Boys' Club out in Flushing, and I wasn't impressed. It was the same shit as tae kwon do except you wore gloves and big shorts and instead of some guy named Tiger Chung Whatever yelling at you, you had some guy named Tito.

"I saw your friend, Peter. He looks just awful. His face is one big bruise, much worse than yours," says Mr. Schnell.

I guess the old guy's seen Diego, though it's a little weird that he's calling that fat bastard my friend. I don't know if it's from his living through the concentration camp, but for a guy who hardly ever says nothing to nobody besides me, the old guy's pretty sharp when it comes to knowing who's down with who on our block.

But then again, the guy's still a grown-up, so of course he's gotta blow things up a little. Sure, Diego had a pretty bad nosebleed. But no one, at least no kid, would ever say his face was all messed up or one big bruise.

"I know this may sound strange right now. But someday you and your friend will both come to regret trying to kill one another."

I doubt that, but I just nod anyway. What else am I gonna do? Stand there and argue with the guy?

"I have a little something for you, by the way, Peter," he says.

I look up. He reaches into his jacket pocket and hands me a beat-up paperback copy of some book called *The Great Gatsby*.

"This, Peter, is a book that's guaranteed to teach you a thing or two about what it means to truly love a woman. I guarantee it will change your life. I can say so with authority because it changed mine when I was your age. Read it and tell me what you think."

It's exactly the same shit he said before he gave me *The Old Man and the Sea*, which was an okay book, I guess, except it felt pretty fucking rotten when the old guy in the book didn't really even catch the fish in the end. I mean, I guess the old guy was pretty brave, but what's the point of going through all that just to drag back a fucking skeleton?

If you ask me, books should be more like *The Count of Monte Cristo*, which has all this intrigue, revenge, and murder, and which Roman got me to read back when we were still friends and used to chill every now and then on his fire escape, which is right below mine. Sometimes, we'd smoke cigarettes or knock down a beer that his mom has lying around the house all the time. But mostly, we'd just chill and shoot the breeze about which girls at school had the best tits besides Linda Rojas.

Other times, we'd sit out there and read, me mostly comic books and him whatever new book he was into. I swear, for a kid who barely passes his classes at school, that kid reads more than any other kid I've ever seen, even the goody-goody Korean kids who live at the library and write 10-page book reports for fun.

Anyway, I don't wanna be rude to Mr. Schnell 'cuz he's done my family a lot of favors over the years and Mom will get on my case if the guy says anything bad about me, so I bite my tongue and just say, "Thanks, Mr. Schnell."

Mr. Schnell just smiles and goes on talking about the book, which is a little weird 'cuz you figure a guy that old wouldn't have much to be excited about.

"With some of these other kids running around here like little hooligans, I know I would be wasting the book. But with you, it's different. I know, Peter, that you can understand and appreciate a good book because you have what it takes."

I just nod. The truth is there's lots of kids who have more of whatever Mr. Schnell's talking about than me. Just take Roman, for instance. But none of the other kids on the block would have anything to do with the old guy 'cuz he's so creepy all the time. I'm not saying Mr. Schnell's some homo who's gonna try to grab your balls like in *Diff'rent Strokes* when Dudley gets molested by the guy from the bike store. But who knows? Mr. De Falco from the A&P looks all normal on the outside, too, but he's a sicko faggot who pays kids to let him suck their dicks with a rubber on. I know 'cuz that's what he offered Roman. So who the hell knows, right?

Anyway, Mr. Schnell reaches inside the front pocket of his suit and takes out this handkerchief that looks like it hasn't been washed in years and blows his snots right into it, before folding it and wiping the sweat off the top of his shiny head. That's another thing with Mr. Schnell. The guy's got the worst fucking hygiene. Like one time, I seen the guy take a swig from a bottle of mouthwash, work it real well around his mouth, then spit it right back into the same bottle. He must have had that bottle of mouthwash for at least 10 years.

Anyway, he then touches my arm and says, "Has your father found a new business for himself?"

I don't know why he's always asking me shit like that. With all the walking around he does, you figure the guy would've seen my dad loafing around the park already. But it never fails. Every time he sees me, the old guy just has to ask me about my dad.

I guess I could make up some bullshit about how Dad got himself a job with some big company in Manhattan and is going to work everyday in a suit. But I don't like lying to the old guy on account of how he seems to see right through me all the time, so I just say, "Not yet, Mr. Schnell."

He nods and says, "Well, don't worry, Peter. With these things, it's all a matter of timing. I'm sure he'll find something soon. He is, after all, still a young man. You mark my words. He will bounce back on his feet in no time. In no time at all."

That's what I used to think, too. But it's been over a year since Dad's lost his store, and all his boxes of rubber boots and crummy fake Pumas are still piled up to the ceiling in our living room. I know that things aren't good right now for a lot of people. But I can't believe how much trouble Dad's having. It's not even like he's an alcoholic or anything like that.

Dad's told me and Steven a hundred times how he started doing the shoe repair store 'cuz it was close to home and that way he could keep an eye on us all the time in case something happened. But sometimes I think it might have been better if Dad had done some vegetable store like Jin and Africa's dads even if it was someplace far like Brooklyn or the Bronx. That way, at least business would be good 'cuz people are always gonna eat oranges, right?

I mean, it was nice of him to keep an eye on us and all that, but the only time we had to call him to come get us from school was during this huge blizzard two years ago. Everyone else's parents had thought to keep their kids home 'cuz there was two feet of snow on the ground. But Mom sent us anyway 'cuz that's just how she is when it comes to school.

Anyway, even though none of the teachers were there, Ms. Veloce, this old white lady who looks like an owl, had us stay in this classroom with these six other kids who'd shown up, too. Of course, they were all total rejects who eat their own boogers and think the teachers are their best friends. I tried to get Ms. Veloce to let me and Steven go home, but she said it was a school rule that no kids could be let out by themselves without a parent or relative picking them up.

Now, some other kid might have just sat there and dealt with the fact that their mom's stupidity had screwed them over and they were stuck with a roomful of booger-eaters while everyone else was outside skitching and bombing cars and playing tackle football. But I just couldn't do it.

So I called Dad from Ms. Veloce's office. Of course, right away, Dad thought I'd done something wrong and gotten in trouble again. But I told him that that wasn't it and explained to him that he had to come get us, only I put it in this way that made it sound like the school was telling him to come get us and he had no choice.

Dad bought it, and 30 minutes later, I could see him waiting outside Ms. Veloce's office as she was walking me and Steven toward him. You should have seen him standing there, patting the snow off his ratty coat. All I could think of was no wonder some old lady gave him a 10-dollar bill once as he was walking home from his store on Christmas Eve.

Everything would have been fine if Ms. Veloce just let us go then, but she had to turn to me and ask, "Is that your father?"

What I said next was pretty rotten. And I kind of regret it now. But at the time, I just couldn't say yes. So I told her he was an uncle.

It didn't matter 'cuz Dad couldn't hear us, and even if he did, he doesn't speak no English. But you should have seen the look Steven gave me. You'd think I'd just stabbed the kid's eye with a pencil or something. I was sure he was gonna rat me out to Dad, but he never did. That's the good thing about the kid. He doesn't yap a lot. Either that or he's real scared of me.

Anyway, it gets me in a sour mood to think about Dad and that time with the blizzard. So I look up at Mr. Schnell and say, "Mr. Schnell, can I ask you something?"

"Sure, Peter? What is it?"

And I tell him about the burglary. It ain't that I think I can get my stuff back. Like I said before, I ain't stupid. I know whoever took my shit's probably pawned it all by now. But I just wanna find out what the hell happened.

And if anyone saw or heard anything, it'd be Mr. Schnell 'cuz the walls in the Holland are paper thin and I know he can hear right into our apartment 'cuz we can hear right into his. Every night at 9:30 he plays the violin for half an hour, nothing but scales over and over. He's offered to teach me a couple of times, but I always come up with some excuse 'cuz the one time I got stuck with the guy in his apartment when I forgot my keys and was locked out, which is when he did that thing with the mouthwash, he talked my ear off about how he used to be some champion boxer in Hungary back in the day. Then he held up his hand and made a fist. I have to admit it was huge, and I can sort of picture Mr. Schnell being a boxer when he was young even though all he ever does now is try to push books on me.

But there's no mention of the guy in any of the books at the library. I know 'cuz I looked it up once. I even asked the librarian for help, which wasn't no fucking picnic 'cuz I don't know what it is about librarians, but they always take one look at me and think I'm up to something. It's the same with gym teachers, which drives me up the wall 'cuz gym's one of the only subjects in school that I actually like.

Maybe Mr. Schnell was just talking out his ass like everyone does once in a while to make it seem like he was some bigshot back in the day. But I don't care. Maybe the guy's never boxed a lick and knows boxing only from watching Rocky chase after chickens. Who gives a shit?

What really bugged me about sitting in that room with him that day was that in the very next breath, he pulls up his sleeve and shows me the numbers tattooed on his forearm and says, "All 15 members of my family were killed by Mr. Adolph Hitler and his SS men in the gas chambers. And all I have left to show for it is this beautiful tattoo."

He said it just like that, then started chuckling like it was some big joke or something. I just sat there, not sure whether to laugh or not. I don't know. Maybe the guy was lying about that, too. But probably not 'cuz his tattoo was real. And who the hell would lie about something like that?

Anyway, after I finish telling him about the burglary, Mr. Schnell doesn't say nothing for a long while. Then he finally says, "I'm very sorry to hear this terrible news, Peter. Your family doesn't deserve such hardship. But now that I know what happened, certain things are becoming more clear to me. I heard yesterday around 5 o'clock many strange noises coming from your apartment."

"What noises?"

"Footsteps and sounds of objects falling down. At first, I thought it was just your parents, Peter, arguing, as they and we all do sometimes. A human being can't help it, cooped up in a box all the time. But these noises didn't stop. They continued for a good 40, 45 minutes. I'm afraid this must have been the burglars." He pauses. "I'm guessing your family lost many things?"

"My Atari with 42 games, my comic book collection, our TV, and my mom's jewelry from her wedding."

"I'm very sorry, Peter. I'm sorry it happened. And I'm sorry I cannot be of more help to you. I didn't know what was going on. Had I known, I would have done something. I assure you. I know it's no outing in the playground to have your home be violated by criminals."

"They went through everything. All the closets and all the drawers. They even took out the cushions on our couch."

"It's the *schvartzes*. It is they who are responsible."

"Who?"

He checks behind him, then says, "Ne-groes," like in all the old hand-me-down books they got at school.

"Black guys?"

He nods. "Black guys."

"You saw them?"

"No, I didn't see them. At least not with my eyes. But I don't have to see. I know. They are lacking in morals and they have no fear of the law. It's a great shame. This used to be a wonderful place to live. Not a place for the wealthy or the bigshots of this city, mind you. But a place for decent hard-working people to raise a family with plenty of German restaurants, some with bowling in the basement. Now there are *schvartzes* and things have changed. I know you don't like to hear that, you and your mother both, but that is the truth even if the truth is a bitter pill to chew."

I nod, more to keep Mr. Schnell quiet than 'cuz I agree with him, even though the old guy does have a point. Not that I'm prejudiced, which I'm not 'cuz I only hate Spanish people and Jewish landlords, but I do know for a fact that a lot of black people do steal. Two kids at Star Lake had fathers who were in jail for holding up gas stations. I know 'cuz the kids told me flat out on the first day like they were proud of it or something.

Anyway, Mr. Schnell gives me a fake punch to the chin and says, "Try not to get too down, Peter. Remember, always keep your chin up. And always remember that things can be taken away from you, but what you have up here." He points to the side of his shiny head. "What you have here is always yours. No one can take that away from you, not the president, not the *schvartzes* and not even the best head shrinker."

From behind Mr. Schnell, Fatty starts giving the Heil Hitler Nazi salute. I know the kid's just trying to be funny, but goddamn! Why's he gotta be so damn retarded for? He could at least wait until the old guy's gone.

I guess Mr. Schnell catches me looking 'cuz he turns around and glares at Fatty. The old guy can make himself look pretty damn mean when he wants to, so good old chickenshit Fatty just smiles a little and plays it off like he's just scratching his head.

Mr. Schnell turns back to me and says, "I like all of your friends, Peter. Even the boy who is mixed. But this boy there, I can't say what it is about him exactly, but something isn't quite right with him."

"It's nothing. He just acts stupid sometimes."

"Again, Peter. I'm very sorry about what happened to you and your family. I don't know what's happening to the world these days. But you mark my words. I'll be sure to talk to the landlord and give him a piece of my mind. It is the responsibility of the landlord to make sure that all tenants in the building are safe and secure. If anyone is responsible, it is him. And he won't get away with it. He may seem to be getting the upper hand now. But you mark my words. His life will be his punishment."

Then, right before he takes off with his empty shopping cart, he gives me the thumbs-up sign and says, like he always does, "You'll be remembered in my will, Peter. That's a promise."

I just stand there and watch the guy for a while. Not that I think he's rich or anything, but I sometimes do wonder if Mr. Schnell really will remember me in his will 'cuz you figure a guy who's Jewish and as old as him has to have some money stashed away somewhere.

But then again, who knows what will happen? Mr. Schnell's so damn crazy, he might die one day and just leave me a bag of marbles or a can of SPAM or another copy of *The Old Man and the Sea*.

No matter what he leaves me or even if he leaves me absolutely nothing at all, I'll always think of Mr. Schnell as a good guy even though he's Jewish and a little nuts for never banging on the walls like the other dickheads on our floor do when my parents fight. As for the books he gives me, in all honesty, my life hasn't changed one bit 'cuz of reading about some old fisherman and I doubt it'll ever change 'cuz of any book 'cuz books are just words and the way I see it, words never changed nothing.

Anyway, as soon as I walk back to where Fatty and Africa are, Fatty says, "Yo, what did that cheap Jew bastard give you this time?"

I hold up the book.

Fatty smiles and says, "Throw that shit in the trash, bro. I got something way better to read."

He then reaches inside the back of his shorts and holds up a copy of *Hustler*. "You guys didn't think all I grabbed was some lousy twin pops, did you?"

It's amazing. I was standing right next to him the whole time at the V&B and I didn't see him grab it. It's like magic, like he should be on *That's Incredible* or *Ripley's Believe It or Not*. I can just picture it. Fatty standing there while the corny white guy says, "Remember, this stunt we're showing is very dangerous. DO NOT attempt this at home!"

Anyway, just like that, I forget all about how Fatty's been annoying the shit out of me the whole morning or how stupid he can be sometimes. None of that matters now. 'Cuz Fatty's the best friend a kid can have and the woman on the cover, whose lips are bright red and whose tits are as big as basketballs, is the most beautiful woman in the whole world. And the only way we can appreciate her true beauty is to worship her in a place where no one can bother us.

CHAPTER 13

WE AIN'T EXACTLY drooling all over ourselves 'cuz it ain't like this is the first dirty magazine we've seen. With Fatty swiping magazines left and right and with Roman's mom letting us watch all those pornos, we pretty much know everything there is to know about sex, like all the different positions and what exactly to say and do to get girls naked and turned on.

But we still can't help grinning like complete morons every time we see a naked girl. That's the power of a naked woman on boys our age. If they had hot naked girls teaching us instead of the dogs and assholes who pass for teachers, all of us would never be late, have perfect attendance, and be on the honor roll. I guarantee it.

Fatty licks his finger and puts it right over the woman's nipples like he's touching the real thing. Then he picks up the magazine and kisses the picture, leaving this wet mark, and says, "You watch, bro. I'm gonna get me a girl just like this when I grow up. Then we're gonna do it three times a day, morning, noon, and night."

I'm just as perverted as the next kid, but Fatty takes the fucking cake. The bastard's got sex on the brain 24-7 and is always begging us to go with him to 42nd Street, so we can look at all the crazy sex gadgets in all the shop windows.

The last time we ditched school and did that, we got caught by this asshole truant officer in less than two minutes while we were staring at this row of dildos in a window. Some of them were as big as my arm. Fatty kept going on about how his was even bigger. But seeing ones that big, even if they're fake, doesn't exactly make you feel too hot about your own, especially after the operation I had last summer with Dr. Min, who's this sketchy doctor who all the Korean parents send their kids to on account of how he charges a third of a regular doctor.

Anyway, on the ride back, we had to sit in this shitty police van with a dozen other horny little morons who'd all had the same idea as us. I guess that just goes to show, there may be a lot of kids in this world, but the stupid ones are always stupid in the same way.

The way my mom whipped me that night with this extension cord, you'd think we'd tried to hold up a bank or something instead of just ditching school on some half day, when we woulda done nothing anyway. That's the thing with her. She seems all quiet and nice on the outside, but she can really lose it sometimes 'cuz she used to be a teacher in Korea, and teachers there can basically beat the shit out of kids and no one even blinks an eye. Which is why I don't even want to think what she'd do if I ever did something really bad like kill somebody or something like that.

Anyway, Fatty flips the page and all of us take a gulp of air, 'cuz even after all the dirty magazines and pornos we've seen, what we see is amazing.

So what's in the magazine?

There's a picture of a naked Chinese girl who kind of looks like one of the girls who used to hang around B.J., touching herself and sucking her fingers at the same time. It's sexy as hell, but also a little weird 'cuz it's the first time I've ever seen a naked Chinese girl.

"Yo, you think her parents know she's in this, bro?" says Fatty.

"Who cares?" I say. All I know is that I have the biggest hardon and I want to jerk off so bad.

"Yo, imagine her dad looks at this. I bet you a hundred dollars that son of a bitch probably jerks off to her and shit."

Like I told you before, Fatty's one sick bastard. And I'm talking *Taboo* and *Faces of Death* sick. I've actually seen the kid pick up used condoms from down by the railroad tracks and smell 'em. And not all of them were dried up, either. Don't ask me why he does it. Who the hell knows?

After we go through every picture in the magazine twice, Fatty sticks it back inside his shorts. Then we wander off to the edge of the roof to smoke cigarettes Fatty swipes off his dad.

Before you start getting all crazy and lecturing me about how cigarettes are bad for you and all that, I know. I ain't stupid. I already took that class in school. But the way I see it, I don't care much one way or the other when it comes to smoking. Dad's tried to tell me a couple of times not to smoke, but he smokes two packs a day, so that should pretty much tell you what I think of his advice. And as bad as you might think smoking is, at least we ain't smoking weed like the whiteboys in Maspeth.

Anyway, while I'm sucking on the cigarette and thinking about all the girls at school I'm gonna try to do it with when school starts again 'cuz there's no way in hell I'm gonna be no god-damn virgin when I start high school, I lean over the roof and look down at everything around us. Even from seven stories up, the place looks like a real shithole.

Old guys like Mr. Schnell are always going on and on about what a nice place Elmhurst used to be back in the day, but you'd never know it by looking at the place now. Except for the Green House, which is this new building with tennis courts on the roof they put up last year where this old abandoned warehouse used to be, there ain't nothing around for blocks and blocks but crummy tenements and black smoke from all the garbage in the incinerators.

For some reason, I start thinking about Ms. Gold, my fifth grade teacher, who's just about the only teacher I ever had who wasn't a complete idiot. Not that I got anything against teachers. They're all right, but 99.99 percent of them's got major attitude problems and would be better off shoveling shit.

But Ms. Gold, who looked kind of like Martina Navratilova, was all right 'cuz she'd always make a big fuss in gym about how fast I could throw. She was also into puzzles like me and hooked me up somehow with a year's subscription to *Games* magazine for just five bucks when it should have cost around twenty. It's 'cuz she's Jewish and has connections. At least that's what my mom said. She's always going on and on about how me and Steven should learn from Jewish people 'cuz they study hard and make a lot of money.

The only thing is, the only Jewish people I know are the teachers at school, Mr. Schnell, and Dad's asshole landlord who wouldn't renew his lease and basically kicked him out of his store. It's because of that greedy penny-pinching Jew bastard that Dad's bumming around the park all the time and we got boxes piled up to the ceiling all over our apartment.

Dad's always going on and on about how the shoes are worth thousands of dollars and he's gonna turn them into cash as soon as he gets another store. He's always going on about how he's gonna turn this or that into cash. Like the time he bought all these fake leather wallets to sell. They looked pretty okay on the outside, I guess. But on the inside they were all crummy and had tags that said *"Made in Itlay."*

If you ask me, you gotta be out of your mind to pay even three bucks for fake Pumas from China that have the stripe going the wrong way and stain your socks blue whenever it rains. Truth is, the shoes are so damn crummy you couldn't even give them away, which only means Steven and me are the only kids in the world who have to wear them all the time.

Another reason I thought Ms. Gold was okay is that she took us on more trips, 13, which is like a school record, than all my other teachers combined. Sure, the trips were to crummy museums, where there ain't nothing to do but walk around and gawk at dinosaur bones, but anything that gets you out of school is all right in my book.

Fact is, the only thing that Ms. Gold had us do that didn't sit right by me was writing to pen pals in Sweden. The girl who wrote to me, Kirsten Something Or Other, was all crazy about disco and roller-skating and automatically thought that I lived in some skyscraper and rode a limousine to school just 'cuz my address said New York. If she only knew the truth. I ain't never been in no limo. Hell, I ain't even been to the Empire State Building.

Still, once when she sent me a picture of herself and she turned out to be pretty, Fatty went berserk. He started hounding me day and night to write all this perverted stuff to her 'cuz he'd heard how Swedish girls are the sluttiest and start doing it when they're 10. I knew that was just more Fatty bullshit. But even if it was true, I just didn't feel like it. And anyway, the girl was way over in some other country. So I sold Fatty the girl's address for five bucks and had him write to her instead. Looking back, I guess that wasn't that cool, but I was sick of writing the girl. I mean, you can't just go on talking about disco and roller-skating and pretending you go around everywhere in some limousines all the time, right?

Anyway, enough about corny pen pals. Fatty walks up to me and tells me to look straight down. I do and see the super waddling out of the building. Even from where we are, there's no mistaking the asshole's square head and the cheap cigar jutting out the jerkoff's mouth. With all the cigars the bastard smokes, you gotta wonder why the dickhead doesn't do the world a favor and just keel over and die already.

Instead, the super goes to his car, pops open the hood, and starts working on it again. It's like that's all the asshole ever does.

"Yo, wouldn't it be good if we had some water balloons, bro?" says Fatty. "We could pee in 'em and throw 'em right on that son of a bitch's head."

It ain't a bad idea. The super deserves to be drenched in pee or puke or worse 'cuz he's always busting our chops for absolutely no fucking reason. So we sometimes play in front of the building. What's the big fucking deal? I mean, it's not like we're knocking into people or snatching purses.

Fact is, we sometimes even hold the door for old ladies going in and out the building. I might even understand if we were kids from a different block, but we fucking live there, don't we? And it ain't like the super even owns the building or anything. He's just there to mop up and take out the garbage while the real owner, this cheap Greek bastard who's so cheap he charges people 50 bucks if they get an air conditioner even though electricity's supposed to be included in our rent's out playing golf and eating gyros. I swear, if I had some guts like B.J., I'd throw a brick down at the super's car. And if the brick happens to miss and hits the super, oh well, like Ms. Gold would say, "T-U-F-F, that spells tough."

"Yo, wouldn't it be funny if it was the super who robbed you, bro?" says Fatty.

I stare at him for a moment. I don't even know where he gets the stuff. Do they write stuff like that up in some secret pamphlet that they hand out only to kids in special ed?

He grins and says, "Just think about it, bro. The super knows exactly when everyone's home or not. And he can go anywhere in the building without anyone ever getting suspicious."

"Stop being stupid, Fatty. I'm not playing around."

"Neither am I. Come on, bro. You saw how that motherfucker stole my ball this morning, didn't you?"

"That's different."

"How's it different? Stealing's stealing, bro. Take it from me. I know. Anyway, it's a proven scientific fact that 85 percent of all supers steal. I read it in the *New York Times*."

"Sure, Fatty."

"I swear to God. The article came out a couple of weeks ago. You can even call them if you don't believe me. All I know is I'd definitely check out the super if I was you."

"Right, just like I should check out the guys from the car wash."

"Make jokes, bro. But if it was my shit that got stolen, I'd check out the super. 'Cuz I'll tell you this much. I know for a fact that he could have got inside your apartment like nothing."

"And how's that, Fatty?"

He looks behind him to make sure no one's around even though we're on the goddamn roof. Then he says, real soft like he's letting me in on some huge secret, "You gotta promise you won't tell nobody."

"Cut the crap and tell me already."

What the bastard says next makes me wonder what planet he's from. I know he's getting left back and I know he's gonna be in special ed, but the kid just ain't got no fucking sense whatsoever.

CHAPTER 14

THERE ARE BAD bullshit artists and good bullshit artists. Then there's Fatty, who'll tell you straight up that two female cops handcuffed him to a chair at the Colony and gave him a handjob without ever batting an eye or anything. Not that I haven't done my share of bullshitting, either. Sure, I'll tell a lie every now and then. But Fatty's something else.

Take the time that Fatty went around telling everyone how B.J. tried to recruit him into the Goblins just before he went to Korea last year. The bastard swears on his grandmother's grave and the Bible and any and every other possible thing to swear on that B.J. asked him, but he had to say no 'cuz he was already down with us Warriors.

Now, the idea of B.J. thinking that anyone else is tough is laughable enough, but B.J. thinking Fatty's tough enough for the Goblins is so ludicrous it ain't even funny. I mean, you've seen just how tough Fatty is.

Anyway, I guess I must be real desperate to even think that Fatty actually knows something about anything. Either that or getting my stuff ripped off has messed up my head like in that book about how this dumb guy gets an operation and becomes smart only to turn stupid again, 'cuz I actually wait for Fatty to tell me how the super could have got inside my apartment.

I'm thinking he's gonna tell me that the super cut a trap door through the ceiling or something like that, but Fatty just says, "The super has a master key."

"A master what?"

Fatty shoots me this look like I'm the moron getting left back and not him.

"A master key, bro. Don't you know nothing? It can open any lock in the city. The cops have it. So do firemen, ambulance guys, and some supers. The mayor gives them out in case of emergencies. My dad applied for one through his store, but he's gotta get clearance from the FBI first. Once everything goes through, though, I'll make us a copy, and then we'll be set."

I search Fatty's face to see if he's joking. For his sake, I hope he is, but the look on his face says he means every single word.

"There's no such thing, Fatty."

"Sure there is. But the government keeps it all hush-hush 'cuz they know everyone would want one and there'd be riots everywhere."

I take a deep breath and remind myself that Fatty's not trying to make me lose it on purpose. It's just how he is. He can't help it that he's stupid. He was just born like that. If anyone's to blame, it's his stupid parents, who've got no one to blame but their stupid parents, and on and on all the way to the first generation. That's why it takes Fatty a week to get things at school that all the other kids figured out a month ago even though his parents send him on Saturdays to some Korean academy out in Flushing where they beat you with a stick if you can't add right.

But all my reminders to myself to stay calm ain't no match for Fatty's stupidity. So I end up shouting anyway.

"Don't be an idiot, Fatty! Whoever told you there was a master key was just messing with you! Goddamn! How stupid can you be?"

He just stares at me for a moment. Then he says, "Fine! Just forget what I said, all right! The hell with you, bro! I was just trying to help."

Fatty shakes his head and starts pouting like some little kid.

I guess maybe I shouldn't yell at him all the time. And I guess he really is trying to help in his own stupid way. But goddamn! Besides there being no such thing as a master key, the super's a worthless dickhead who's got shit for brains, so there's just no way in hell he could've pulled off a robbery. You gotta have some guts and at least half a brain to rob houses, and the super doesn't even have that. If he did, you can bet he wouldn't be pushing no mop around or driving around in no 25-dollar piece of shit.

Anyway, I lean out over the edge of the roof and look down at the super again. He's bent over under the hood of his car, so all we can see are his legs jutting out. If we threw down a brick, or better yet, a refrigerator, it would crush the hood and chop the super in half, like a guillotine.

Then it hits me, and for a moment I just stand there and wonder why I didn't think about it sooner. That's the thing with me. Once in a while, I'll get these ideas that are just so good that I wonder what my brain's doing the rest of the time.

'Cuz maybe we don't got a brick or a refrigerator, but that don't mean we gotta just stand there like morons and miss out on a God-given chance to teach the super a lesson he'll never forget.

CHAPTER 15

STICKBALL, HANDBALL, MANHUNT, and kick-the-can are all good games. But like all games, you can only play them so much before you get bored shitless. Even war, where we fling rocks and bottles down by the railroad tracks, gets old pretty fast. But pin-the-tail-on-the-fucking-super's a game I could play forever.

We're seven floors up, but we can hear the super bang his head against the hood when the jumping jacks go off right next to his car. It's like the asshole's head's made of metal 'cuz it sounds like someone hit a gong.

I guess technically, someone might say we're picking on a cripple who's also mentally retarded, but who the fuck cares? You've already seen what we did to the tard car. Anyway, the bastard deserves it. He's been messing with us forever just 'cuz we're kids. And it's 'cuz of him that we gotta sneak around our own building like fucking roaches.

Once all the jumping jacks go off, the douchebag looks up at the roof and shouts, "Who's there? Who's up on the roof?"

It's like the dumb fuck actually expects us to shout down an answer. That's the thing with Puerto Ricans. I don't know if it's all the *platanos* they eat or all their cha-cha-cha music, but they think just like monkeys.

But a stupid question always deserves a stupid answer. So me, Fatty, and Africa open our flies and take a seven-story leak that rains down right at the worthless dumb fuck. With all three of us peeing, it's like there's a small waterfall all of a sudden, except there's no ferry and no one going down on a barrel.

The super limps out of the way, but not fast enough to get out of the spray that bounces off the ground. Then he waves his fist and mutters some curses in Spanish, before waddling back into the building.

Whether the fucking jerkoff takes the elevator or comes up the stairs, it'll take more than two minutes 'cuz of his gimp leg, which is plenty of time for us to get the hell out of there. We can go down any of the fire escapes that run along the front and back of the building. But that's probably what the super expects us to do. And for all we know, the sneaky fuck could be hiding inside the lobby, just waiting for us to come down, so he can pop back out and nab us.

So instead of going down, we go up. Up the block, that is, past a whole row of busted TV antennas and Fruit of the Looms with dingleberry stains hanging off clotheslines from all the old ladies who're too cheap to spring for the quarter dryers at the laundromat. Sure we're leaving shoe prints everywhere 'cuz the tar under us is soft and squishy. But it don't matter none 'cuz the super could never put two and two together, and there's no way in hell he can clear the four feet of space between our building and the one next to us.

Me, Fatty, and Africa all jump across. But Steven just stands there and gives me this look like he'd rather die than jump.

His baby act might work with Mom and Dad, but it sure as hell ain't gonna work with me. So I look right at him and shout, "I ain't playing, Steven. Get over here now!"

He pouts a little, then jumps across, clearing the roof by more than a foot, which just goes to show you the kid could have done it all along and should have done it from the beginning. That's the thing with the kid sometimes. I don't like pulling rank on the kid, and I usually don't on account of how sickly he is. But he's gotta learn that if I want him to do something, he better do it. That's just how things work. I'm the older brother, so he's gotta listen to what I say. Otherwise, he'll grow up soft and spoiled like some stupid dipshit who thinks everybody's their best friend.

A minute later, we're climbing down the fire escape of the building that leads to a back alley behind the car wash that none of the grown-ups even knows is there. It's about as clean a getaway as there is. The only thing is, halfway down all of us can't help but stop and stare with our mouths open 'cuz what we see below us is more shocking than seeing people scooping out monkey brains or clubbing the shit out of some seals. It's something so unfucking-believable that not a single one of us would have dreamed it was possible in a million fucking years.

CHAPTER 16

I GUESS THIS IS as good a time as any to tell you about Star Lake, 'cuz I keep talking about it and maybe you're confused. That name may sound like some fancy sleepaway camp, where rich kids go to ride horses and take sailing lessons, but it was really this place that Mom found out about from this commercial on TV that had all these happy white kids with rosy cheeks hiking up some mountain straight outta *The Sound of Music*, which is Mom's favorite movie. What can I tell you? She's all corny like that. But then again, most other moms I know wouldn't have even thought to call the number, but Mom's always got all these crazy ideas. Take how she used to tell me and Steven how she's gonna send us one of these summers to some boarding school in Canada that's run by nuns so we can learn French and become trilingual with English and Korean. I don't know where Mom gets all her weird ideas, but I know it's got to do with the fact that she's educated and was the first person in her family to go to college. The rest of her family mostly either finished just elementary or junior high school 'cuz they weren't that smart and couldn't afford it. I know 'cuz Mom's told me. She was smart and got scholarships. She even went to the Philippines to study English for a year after she finished college. That's why she doesn't sound all stupid when she talks like Fatty or Africa's moms, who all just got married straight out of high school and got knocked up, or got knocked up then got married. Either way, they're retards compared to Mom. Which is why as crummy as our apartment is there are books there, not like Fatty's house, where there are just four books, all dusty textbooks from school.

Anyway, Mom called the number on the screen and the lady on the other end signed Steven and me up for two weeks of sleepaway camp for 30 bucks apiece. That should have clued us in. But we didn't find out until we went to get on the bus in this part of

Manhattan that was all burnt up, that the camp was actually run by the Salvation Army for pretty much every poor black kid in the city.

I guess it was weird for me and Steven to be there 'cuz every single kid there and their parents was staring at us like what the hell were we doing there, which was what I was wondering, too. It was so bad that Mom—who's always telling me and Steven about Gandhi and Martin Luther King and how we shouldn't be prejudiced against black people and all that 'cuz God made us all the same, only white people came out of the oven too soon and black people came out too late—actually pulled me and Steven aside and asked us if we wanted to go back home and skip the two weeks. She even offered to give us money, which just shows you how freaked out she was.

Now, some other kid might have said yes, let's go home, and maybe that's what I should have done, too. But I didn't. Not that I like being the only Chinese kid in a camp full of a thousand black kids, which sounds like the beginning of some joke, but I just didn't want to get back in our crummy station wagon after being so excited about going away some place and just come back home, especially after I'd talked up the camp to Fatty and the rest of my friends for weeks and weeks. Talk about your duds. That would have been the dud of all duds.

So I said no, and me and Steven got on that bus. And for the next two weeks, I fought an average of six times a day—twice in the morning, twice at lunch, and twice after dinner—whenever and wherever some stupid black kid looked at me the wrong way and said anything that sounded even remotely Chinese. Of course, once they saw that I wasn't no sissy and could handle my own, they wised up and started ganging up on me, which was fine by me 'cuz I always like fighting against crazy odds. The only bad part was at night, when I had to sleep with one eye open 'cuz you could never tell when some punk would sneak up on you with chains or brass knuckles. But I did it. And I fucking kicked all their asses and taught every single one of them never to mess with nobody from Elmhurst or the Warriors 'cuz we're the baddest.

At least, that's the story I told when I came back. The truth is a little different.

Sure, a lot of kids at Star Lake were from bad neighborhoods, and like in any other place with a thousand kids, there definitely were a couple of nut jobs. Like this kid Howard, who'd cut up his palm with a razor blade, then sew it back up with a regular needle and thread for fun. Then there was Nathaniel, who kept peeing in his bed every night until Dr. Doom, our counselor, this crazy black guy who never said a word during the two weeks and just lay up on the rafters in his sunglasses reading comic books all the time, got fed up and sent his ass packing in the middle of the night with all his shit stuffed in two milk crates.

I got a couple of ching-chongs and kids kept coming up to me and Steven all the time and asking if we were lost, but most of the kids left me alone. Honestly, I had maybe *one* fight during the entire two weeks, and Dr. Doom flew down from the rafters and broke that up before it even started. Why did they leave me alone? Partly it was 'cuz of this rumor, which I swear I didn't start, that I was a black belt in karate. Partly it was 'cuz of the Rubik's Cube. That's another thing I forgot to tell you about myself. I'm not bragging or anything, but I'm something of a wiz when it comes to solving puzzles, which is why me and Ms. Gold got along so well.

Now, I'm not gonna try to tell you that learning to do the Rubik's Cube was easy. 'Cuz it wasn't. It took me a full six months, and I almost got fed up with it and gave up lots of times. But I stuck it out, which just goes to show you how stubborn my mom and dad have made me. Anyway, I know that doing the Rubik's Cube ain't the hardest thing in the world. But except for the kids who came out on TV, I've yet to see any other kid do it. Sure, there are lots of kids who say they can do it, but most of them just peel the stickers off or take the cube apart. So, yeah, next to being able to throw fast, I guess being able to do the Rubik's Cube is something that I'm pretty proud of.

Anyway, the guy who ran the camp, this skinny old black guy with gray hair named Dr. Washington, thought it was a pretty big deal, too. So he got everyone to call me Mr. Rubik and even had me do it in front of everyone at the Star Lake Talent Show, which was on the last night of the camp. I guess I was a little nervous 'cuz I had to go on right after these kids who did this real badass break-dance routine. So I started messing up in the middle, and a couple of kids sitting in the front row kept shaking their heads and saying, "He ain't gonna do it. He ain't gonna do it."

But then I recovered and started doing this thing I do, where I look up at the ceiling and not even look at the cube when I'm pretty close to finishing it. Yeah, I know it's showing off, but I wanted to show up those kids who'd said I couldn't do it.

When I was done, Dr. Washington, who was timing me with this stopwatch, called out, "A minute and 12 seconds. I guess Mr. Rubik was a little nervous tonight 'cuz I've seen him do it in a lot less."

I'll never forget what happened next 'cuz there was all this applause, even from the kids in the front who'd said that I couldn't do it. And then, as I was walking back to my seat, Dr. Doom, who never said a word to me the whole time I was there, slapped my back and said, "Good job, Mr. Rubik."

I know this is gonna sound super corny, but I swear. Apart from being born, which I don't remember at all, and when I finally have sex, which will hopefully be some time this year, that night at Star Lake might have been the best fucking moment of my life.

Anyway, looking back, I'm kind of glad I said no to my mom and went to Star Lake even though it was with a whole bunch of black kids, 'cuz I learned four important things about life: 1) Black kids can't swim. 2) Black kids got outies instead of innies. 3) If some mean-looking black kid ever asks you if you know karate, the best thing to do is to say nothing and just make the kid wonder. 4) Basketball and football's okay if you're into running and all that, but the baddest thing any kid can do anywhere is breakdance.

Which is why it makes no sense now, that Hindu Tim, a total wuss, whose best friend is a dog-faced girl Steven's age and who used to go around asking us if we wanted to borrow money from him, is doing the handspin. I don't know how long he's been practicing in secret like that, but it's like when that wimpy guy in *Master Killer* goes to Shaolin Temple to learn all 35 chambers 'cuz

I swear to God, the kid's not bad. I'm not saying he's as good as the kids at Star Lake or that he's ready to battle at USA, where kids pull off no-handed windmills like nothing, but he's actually break-dancing and not just flopping around and making an ass of him-self like when Fatty starts breakdancing.

I guess every one of us is stunned 'cuz none of us makes a sound as Hindu Tim comes out of a backspin into this pose where he grabs his chin and his crotch at the same time. It doesn't look half bad, especially 'cuz the kid's all decked out in shelltops, fat laces, and even a gold chain with a *Playboy* medallion like they sell in Chinatown. I don't care about the shelltops, but the chain is dope. It's what I'd get for myself if I had the money.

Fatty starts clapping real loud, then jumps down off the fire escape. Hindu Tim crawls up off the ground, and tries to run for it. Who knows why he starts running? The kid's just all stupid and scared like that. Not that it does him any good 'cuz he's the slow-est kid on the block, even slower than Steven or Diego. He'll tell you it's 'cuz he's got too many muscles in his calves, but you know it's gotta be something else, like the Hindu flu or something like that.

Anyway, Fatty nabs the kid before he takes 20 steps, then puts him in a headlock in less than half a second. "What the fuck you running for, Shitstain?" he says, calling the kid by his favorite nickname and twisting the kid's head hard to one side.

It's like we're watching Bob Backlund battling the Iron Sheik, except without no chicken-wing or no camel-clutch.

"Let go of me," says Hindu Tim, in this super whiny voice of his, trying to hit Fatty's back with his arms even though it's no use. Fatty just yanks his head even harder so that his shirt rides up his back and we get a good look at all the nasty hair above his butt crack. It's like the kid's parents were Bigfoots like in that Eddie Murphy tape, where they go *"Agoony-goo-goo."*

"So this is what you do all the time, hunh, Shitstain?" says Fatty.

"Get off me."

It ain't that we enjoy picking on Hindu Tim. We just think it's a lot of fun to watch the kid squirm and get all scared. I don't know where the dickweed used to live, but it must have been one soft place 'cuz since moving to the Holland, the kid's made a name for himself as one of the wussiest kids ever. For the longest time, the kid didn't have a single friend 'cuz everyone just kind of abused him and ranked him out all the time on account of what a scrub he was. But then again, you can't help but feel a little sorry for the kid sometimes. Sure he's weak and soft and all that. But a big reason why he's such a wuss is 'cuz he's the only Hindu on the block. Who knows? If there were a whole bunch of Hindus around, even Hindu Tim might be a completely different kind of kid.

Anyway, Fatty tightens the headlock and says, "You're one funny Hindu, you know that? You think just 'cuz you can do backspins, you're down? Breakdancing's not for fucking Hindus. So don't even try it."

"Get off me."

"After you answer this question, Shitstain. Did you see anybody carrying stuff out our building yesterday?"

"What?" says Hindu Tim, all confused.

I shoot Fatty a look. The fucking bastard's got such a big mouth. Next thing you know, the fatass will be telling my business to all the loony tunes from the Leben Home.

"Just answer the fucking question, you dumb fuck. Did you see anybody carrying anything outta the building yesterday?" says Fatty.

"No."

"Think hard, you fuck. Or we'll call the Dotbusters on your ass."

"I didn't see nobody carrying nothing. I swear."

"Let him go, Fatty," I say.

Fatty lets go of the headlock, then sweeps Hindu Tim's feet and throws him down on the ground.

Hindu Tim gets up slowly, then just stares at us like he's scared we're gonna kill him or something.

"Don't be scared, Tim. We ain't gonna kill you or nothing," I say.

"I ain't scared," he says.

I try not to laugh. Every fucking kid's gotta try to be a tough guy.

"You seen Jin today?" I say.

"Yeah, I saw him."

"When?"

"A little while ago. The super was yelling at him for something, then he just went walking up the block." He pauses. "It looked like someone beat him up."

"What the fuck you talking about, you fucking Hindu?" says Fatty.

"It looked like he got beat up. He had all these bruises on his face."

The first thought that pops into my head is that maybe Diego and his cousin got to Jin to get back at me. That's what it means to be down with a crew. Sometimes, you get jumped just 'cuz someone's got beef with your crew.

"He's lying, bro," says Fatty. "This fucking Hindu's messing with us for no reason."

"I'm not lying. I know what I saw. He had bruises all over his face. You can even ask your friend Roman. He was there. He saw it, too."

"Stop talking out your ass, you freaking Hindu," says Fatty. "Nobody fucking touched Jin."

"Then how come he's got all those bruises?" says Hindu Tim.

"He ain't got no bruises. And you better stop lying 'cuz I'll kick your ass for real. I'll knock you upside the head so hard so fast, you'll wish your parents never prayed to that fucking cow."

"Cut it out, Fatty," I say.

"He's fucking lying to us, bro."

"Just stop it, all right."

Fatty shakes his head, then goes and starts ripping up the cardboard box that Hindu Tim was breakdancing on. I don't know why the kid's gotta be so damn stupid for. It ain't like Hindu Tim can't just go find himself more boxes.

I turn back to Hindu Tim and say, "You're sure he had bruises on his face?"

"Yeah, I'm sure."

I stand there and think about what he just said. If it's true, it means either Diego fucked him up to get back at me or Jin got jumped by some dickhead whiteboys from Maspeth. Either way, we gotta find the kid and talk to him.

"What's all this about anyway? How come you guys are asking all these weird questions?" says Hindu Tim.

"Mind your own fucking business," says Fatty.

I look over at him almost in shock. I woulda never thought Fatty could keep his mouth shut about anything.

But Fatty doesn't let me down. In the very next breath, he says, "If you really wanna know, you fuck, Peter's apartment got robbed. They took his Atari and his TV."

Hindu Tim looks at me and says, "I'm sorry, man. That's messed up."

"It ain't nothing. Don't worry about it," I say, then give Fatty the evil eye. Thanks to his big mouth, I even got fucking wusses like Hindu Tim feeling sorry for me.

"You think it was someone from the building?" says Hindu Tim.

"I don't know. If you see Jin again, tell him we're looking for him, all right?"

He nods.

Then, just as we're about to cut out of there, Hindu Tim says, "Pete, I almost forgot."

"What?"

"Diego told me to tell you you guys are dead 'cuz his cousin's crazy."

I stare at him. It's not that the kid's exactly smiling or nothing, but something about the way he said that ticks me off. I mean, even if that's what Diego told him to say, why the fuck does he have to do what Diego tells him to?

So I get right in his face and say, "Man, fuck you. Who the fuck you think you are talking shit to me like that?"

"I was just . . ."

"Shut the hell up! What are you, Diego's fucking messenger boy? Man, I bet you'd probably side with him and his cousin if we fought him."

"I wouldn't. I would side with you guys." He takes a step back, and his *Playboy* medallion dangles off his chest.

"Bullshit."

"I swear. I wouldn't side with Diego. He's a dick."

"Stop lying. You're fucked up, man. I try to be nice to you even though you're a Hindu, and you fucking start with me for no reason. Man, what the fuck is wrong with you?"

"I'm sorry. I didn't mean . . ."

"Forget you. Sorry ain't gonna do it, man. This is beyond sorry. You fucking dissed me."

"I'm sorry."

"I didn't wanna do this. But you give me no choice. Give me your fucking chain."

His mouth opens, but he doesn't say nothing.

"What the fuck you just standing there for? Give it up."

"This isn't worth anything. I got it for two dollars."

"Then give the shit up already. Come on, man. We ain't got all day."

"Give the shit up!" says Fatty.

Hindu Tim looks over at Africa and Steven like he wants them to step in. But it's no use. They just stand there.

I know I'm being a dick, but it's Hindu Tim's own damn fault. He shouldn't have said that shit about Diego and his cousin.

"I'm not gonna say it again, Tim. Give it up."

That's all it takes. He takes the chain off and hands it to me.

"That's better," I say. "Next time, you make sure you don't start with me. And don't fucking act like you're Diego's messenger boy. 'Cuz you're not. You're down with us, not him."

I then hold out my hand so he can slap it, but he just stares at it.

"Come on, Tim. You gonna leave me hanging?"

He finally slaps my hand.

"We're cool, right?" I say.

He nods.

"Good. Now keep practicing, man. You're pretty good. Way better than Fatty."

And just like that, the kid actually breaks into a smile. But that don't last long 'cuz right before we cut out for real to look for Jin, Fatty says, "Yo, tell your sister not to wear no panties tonight 'cuz I'm gonna come by and fuck her later."

You should see the way Hindu Tim stares at us. It's like he's making some list in his head so he can hunt us down one by one and get back at us someday.

But the hell with him. He can make a thousand lists and become the best breakdancer in the world. As long as he stays a pussy, nothing's gonna stop him from getting fucked.

CHAPTER 17

THERE'S NO SIGN of Jin anywhere. Not the arcade, the bowling alley, or the pool hall. No one's seen the kid. It's like the kid's gone m.i.a. on us and up and vanished like some fucking ninja.

We even go down to the railroad tracks 'cuz who knows? Maybe the kid's there, having himself a grand old time, jumping off trees onto old mattresses, breaking bottles, or setting fires.

But there's no sign of the guy. And all we see's some dead dog on the tracks that looks like it's been rotting there for weeks.

"Looks like throw-up spaghetti, don't it?" says Fatty, poking a stick at the slimy maggots in its stomach.

Nobody but Fatty would think of that, especially since the air smells so gross and there are all these nasty little bugs swarming all around us. But then again, the maggots do kind of look like that.

Fatty pokes the maggots again and says, "I had a dream just like this the other day, bro. We were all down here in the railroad tracks just like this, checking out a dead dog. Except in the dream, the dog came back to life as a cannibal and started eating people. I'm telling you. It's déjà vu, bro. Déjà fucking vu!"

I don't know where he picked up that word, but I know we're gonna hear it from him all day now.

He shoves the stick deeper, then says, "Check out these maggots, bro. They had maggots just like these in my grandma's bathroom. You guys should have seen it, bro. Her toilet was just a hole in the ground filled with like 10 years' worth of shit and piss. Whenever it looked like it was about to fill up and flood, they had this guy come around to take the shit away in buckets. That was the guy's shitty job." He pauses. "Get it? Shitty job?"

"You're corny, Fatty," says Africa.

"Shut your ass. And tell your mom to give you a real haircut instead of that same old bowl cut you've had all your life."

They both flip each other the bird. Then Fatty looks over at me and says, "So how d'you think it died, bro?"

"I don't know, Fatty. Maybe it got hit by the train," I say, more to shut him up than 'cuz I'm really interested. It's dead. And no amount of bullshitting about how it died's gonna bring it back to life, right?

Of course, Fatty doesn't think so. He says, "You think so? I was thinking maybe some crazy bum killed it for food. Like the way they do in Korea. My dad ate dogs all the time when we went to Korea last summer. He got me to eat it, too. It was nasty, bro. They put the dog in this sack and beat it with baseball bats for like an hour until it dies. The dog just barks and cries the whole time. I didn't think I could eat it, but it's good for your you-know-what so you can do it for hours."

I just stare at Fatty, wondering how the hell the kid can think about doing it when we're two feet from a rotting dog and the air's so nasty we can barely breathe.

"I'm stuck here this summer, bro, 'cuz fucking Ms. Waters failed me. But I'm gonna go to Korea next summer for sure. My uncle's gonna hook me up, bro. He's got it all set up with this friend of his from the army who works at this TV station. Then I'll be rapping and breakdancing over there, and doing it with tons of girls. They throw their panties at you, bro."

"Man, shut the fuck up. You can't even breakdance as good as Hindu Tim," I say.

"You're bugging. I'm the best breakdancer around. They even tried to get me to be in *Beat Street*, but I turned them down, bro."

"In your fucking dreams. You can't even do the worm."

"Yeah? Then how come people are on my dick and begging me to breakdance at USA?"

"No one's begging you for shit."

"You'll see, bro. I'm gonna breakdance there next week. My boy Quick's gonna be the deejay. Him and Afrikaa Bambataa and all these other guys from Zulu Nation."

"Yeah right, Fatty."

"Like I been telling you all day, bro, you can believe me or not. I know I'm fly. And what's more important, so do the ladies."

He smiles to himself, then shoves the stick so deep it's like he's trying to make himself a Korean shish kebab.

"Leave it alone, Fatty!" Steven screams all of a sudden in this super high voice he gets when he's really upset about something.

I hadn't really noticed until now, but the kid looks totally messed up, like he's about to cry or something. Who knows why, but I guess the dead dog's really freaking him out.

Fatty shakes his head and says, "What the hell's the matter with you, kid?"

"Stop hurting it," says Steven.

"I ain't hurting it, stupid. It's already dead. How you gonna hurt something that's already dead? Don't you know nothing about nothing?"

Steven looks up at me and tugs my arm. "Make him stop, Peter. Please."

It's no big deal to me what Fatty does to the dog. He can eat it, blow it up, or hump it for all I care. It's already dead, and there ain't nothing the bastard can do to it that's worse than that.

Still, it's freaky to see Steven so worked up about something 'cuz usually the kid won't say a word about nothing. Take when I fought Diego and took the chain off Hindu Tim. I know the kid was upset, but you didn't see the kid acting all weird like he's doing now, right?

So I turn to Fatty and say, "Stop already, Fatty. Can't you see you're freaking the kid out?"

"Damn, bro. It's only a dead dog, for crying out loud. It ain't like it's a dead person or nothing."

"Just do me a favor and stop. All right? The kid's about to cry."

Fatty rolls his eyes, then makes a huge deal of yanking the stick out of the dog and chucking it into the bushes like he's doing me the biggest favor in the world. As soon as the stick hits the ground, there's a rustling sound like a whole bunch of rats are scurrying away.

Fatty then turns to Steven and says, "What the hell's the matter with you, hunh? If you freak out this bad just because of some stupid dead dog, what the hell are you gonna do when you see a dead person? A dead person's a hundred times more nasty than this. Their eyes get all puffed up. Their skin gets all stretched out. And their eyeballs start melting. What the hell you gonna do then, hunh?"

Steven grabs my arm like he's really scared. And fucking Fatty starts laughing like he's getting a kick out of scaring the kid.

So I say, "You're full of shit, Fatty. You don't know shit about no dead person 'cuz you ain't never seen one. So shut the hell up."

"I have, too."

"Yeah, right. In your fucking dreams."

"Not in my dreams, bro. In real life. I've seen lots of dead people. Shit, people get killed outside my parents' store all the time. That's how things are in Brooklyn. Compared to Brooklyn, Elmhurst is soft. Shit, I bet you guys wouldn't last 10 minutes over there."

"Shut the fuck up. All you ever do is talk out your fat ass."

"Yeah? You think so?"

"I know so."

"Fine. How 'bout this, then? Three days ago, these two guys in ski masks came into my parents' store with shotguns. They put the guns right in my mom's head and nearly blew her head off before they took off with all the money in the cash register. How about that, hunh? You still think I don't know what I'm talking about? You ain't the only one who's been robbed, bro."

I stare right at Fatty's shiny round head, wondering what the hell's wrong with the kid. He looks just like any other fat kid. But why the hell's he gotta lie all the time for? I've never been to his parents' crummy store, but I just know things there can't be as bad as Fatty says. It was the same with Star Lake. Things are never as bad or scary as people make 'em out to be.

"Fine, Fatty. If you've seen so many dead people, then this dog doesn't scare you at all, right?"

"Hell no, bro. This dog don't do shit to me."

"Then I dare you to touch it."

He clears his throat and spits a fat loogy into the bushes. "What the fuck for? Why the hell would I want to touch this nasty thing, bro?"

"To prove how brave and tough you are. Do it for Brooklyn. Do it for your homeboy Quick."

"Forget you, bro. I don't gotta prove nothing."

"Maybe that's 'cuz you ain't got the guts. Maybe that's 'cuz you ain't nothing but talk."

"Go to hell, bro."

"Go to hell, bro," I mimic in a chickenshit whiny voice. Then I say, back in my regular voice, "You don't even have to touch it. Just put your hand near it. I bet you can't even do that 'cuz you're so damn scared."

"I ain't scared of nothing."

"You can't do it, Fatty, 'cuz you're scared and you ain't never seen no dead body or nobody in no ski masks and your mom never got her head almost blown off. You can't do it 'cuz none of that stuff about Brooklyn you're always going on and on about is true."

He stares at me like he's about to start swinging, then says, "You don't know shit, bro."

"Come on, then. What're you scared of? All you gotta do is hold out your hand like this."

I crouch down and hold out my hand, so that there's a foot of space between it and the maggots.

Fatty stares at me for a long while, then says, "Fine."

He puts his hand out next to mine, then says, "You happy now?"

"Lower," I say, dropping my hand a couple of inches.

Fatty rolls his eyes and sighs, then puts his hand lower than mine.

"Lower," I say again, then dip my hand a few inches so it's lower than Fatty's.

And stupid Fatty lowers his hand.

And it's all over. I grab the bastard's wrist with both hands and push his hand right into the squishy mess and hold it there while the maggots start squirming.

Fatty tries to yank his hand out, but I got two hands on him, so it's no use.

When I finally let go of his hand, Fatty doesn't say a word. He just goes over to a bush and starts puking his guts out. It sounds like he's throwing up his last six meals.

Then, when he's finally done upchucking, he shakes his head and shoots me the dirtiest look ever, like I just ratted him out to the principal or something.

He then turns around and goes down the dirt path back out to the street. Even after yakking his guts out, the bastard's still gotta strut like he's some badass.

I guess maybe I shouldn't have pushed his hand into the dog, but I don't exactly feel bad for him. The bastard deserves it. He shouldn't have gone on and on all morning about Brooklyn and what a badass he is. And he shouldn't have yapped to everyone about my apartment getting ripped off.

CHAPTER 18

THE PLAYGROUND'S SUPPOSED to be only for customers and kids who are there with their parents. At least, that's what the sign on the front gate says. But the geniuses who work there are too busy to notice nothing. They got more important things to worry about like figuring out how many ketchups to hand out with each order and how to get people to stop going to the McDonald's down the street. Personally, I prefer a Whopper to a Big Mac any day, but even dumbasses gotta eat too, right?

Anyway, there's some stupid lady downing fries with her two kids at the picnic table at the other end who looks like she could be Ms. Gold's identical twin except that her ass is twice as big.

The stupid cow doesn't know us from a pile of beans, but she still gives us the evil eye like she's just waiting for us to do something bad even though we're not doing a damn thing. We ain't flinging rocks. We ain't spitting on the handrails. We ain't even spilling nothing down the slide.

Still, the fat-assed hag probably thinks we're in some gang and out to beat the shit out of her kids. Maybe we would, if she weren't there, just to let them know they ain't nothing special.

Africa ducks inside to check on Fatty in the bathroom, and I go over to the fence and look out at Queens Boulevard. Some old guy who looks a little like Mr. Schnell's trying to cross the street, but it's impossible 'cuz there's 10 lanes of cars, and not one single car's doing the speed limit. It's like Frogger except there's no moving logs and the old guy can't hop at all, which gets me thinking how the world would be a better and safer place if everyone drove the speed limit and waited for old people every now and then.

Bullshit!

As soon as I get my license, I'm getting me a Porsche and all the motherfuckers on the road can eat my dust 'cuz there's no way in hell you'll ever catch me in no crummy station wagon.

Africa comes back out, giggling to himself. So I ask him what's so funny and he says, "I think Fatty's in there taking a dump."

We both start laughing 'cuz if anyone would take a dump then, it'd be Fatty. And we know 'cuz he's always telling us about his dumps. I swear. Fatty's the only kid I know who can talk your ear off for hours about the kind of shit he took. He'll not not only tell you how big it was, but what was in it—like whether it was bits of lettuce or carrots. In fifth grade, he once took a dump that was so huge that it clogged up the toilet and flooded the bathroom right outside the cafeteria. Tiny shit drops were floating all over the place. Kids were running around screaming. And a couple of lunch aides almost fucking fainted.

When we finally stop laughing, Africa reaches inside his pocket and takes out two Burger King game cards, the kind they're only supposed to give out to customers.

"How'd you get those?" I say.

He just shrugs, then hands me one. That's the cool thing about Africa. If it'd been Fatty, he would've run his mouth for 20 minutes telling you how he kicked some big black guy's ass to get the fucking game cards.

I fish a nickel out of my pocket and scratch off the three silver circles on my card. If we're lucky, we might win a free cheeseburger or maybe even a Coke.

But my card's a dud. And so's Africa's. Underneath the silver circles, it just says, *"Please Try Again."*

It might as well tell us to go fuck ourselves.

Africa tears up his card and chucks the pieces on the ground. I'm about to do the same when Steven rushes over to me from the swing and puts out his hand.

"This card's no good. We didn't win nothing," I say to the kid.

But the kid just smiles like he couldn't care less. I don't know why, but every single person in my family's a stubborn son of a bitch. So what can I do? I hand it to him, and he runs back to the swing, which is just an old truck tire hanging off three metal chains.

I don't know. I know Steven's not dumb like Fatty, but he acts so weird and retarded sometimes. I mean, the kid just doesn't make any kind of sense at all. What the hell's he want a game card that's no good for?

Africa stares at me and says, "It's okay, Pete. He's just little. That's all."

I nod, even though that's not true. Then I pick up a small rock and fling it over the fence that faces out to Dongan at this lamppost. It misses wide by 10 yards and lands in the Merit station across the street.

I guess it's good that Africa's always trying to be nice to the kid and all that, but I gotta admit it gets annoying sometimes 'cuz it's almost like he's trying to show me up or something. I never said I was a good brother. But then again, it ain't like I'm a bad brother, neither. I mean, I ain't ever really mean to the kid. And I don't yell at the kid and I don't pound on him for no reason like some other older brothers do. Fact is, I've never laid a hand on the kid. Show me any other older brother who can say that. I dare you.

Africa kicks a paper cup on the ground toward the fence, then says, "You think you'll do another paper route to get another Atari?"

"What for? So someone can come steal that one, too?"

He doesn't say nothing. Neither do I. The only sound is the cars racing past us from Queens Boulevard and the squeaking from Steven's swing.

"You kids can't be in here!"

We turn around and see some dumbass Burger King employee who's got on a stupid paper hat to go with his even cooler uniform.

"You kids can't be here!" he shouts again as he comes right up to us. The guy looks like he's thirty, but has a ton of pimple scars on his face like all he did as a kid was jerk off and pick at his zits.

I look him right in the eye and say, "We're waiting for my mom. She told us to wait for her here."

"Don't get smart with me, you little wiseass. Who do you think you're talking to? I wasn't born yesterday!"

I never said he was. And I guess I was being wise, but it still doesn't feel right that the guy doesn't give me the benefit of the doubt. After all, the guy doesn't know me from a rat's ass, and I am a kid. And I do have a mom.

"You kids got no business being in here. See the sign. This playground's only for customers. You gotta get out of here right now!" he shouts, then starts herding us out toward the exit like we're cows.

Of course, Ms. Gold's fake fat-assed twin's got this look on her face like she's so pleased with her damn self 'cuz she just couldn't wait to see us get kicked out. I so wanna shove my foot right up her fat ass. So as we walk past her, I shout, "What the hell you looking at, you fat-assed bitch!"

She makes a face like she's never been so insulted in her life and pulls her kids closer to her like they might get contaminated just by being near us.

Like mother, like daughters. The two kids look like real wusses, like they'll grow up to be complete homos who wear pink pants and get manicures and wet their pants for Menudo.

The douchebag from Burger King gives me one final shove out to the sidewalk and says, "If I ever see you here again, I'm calling the cops!"

What a tough guy. He's probably 30-something making three bucks an hour. And he's gotta threaten us with cops.

"Fuck you, asshole! Call the cops! See what they do for your fucking ass!"

CHAPTER 19

THE HINDU INSIDE the metal booth at the Merit station keeps giving us dirty looks, but doesn't step out to chase us away. The guy's probably all scared like he thinks we got guns and are about to stick him up or something.

"You wanna go to USA later? It's penny night tonight," says Africa, all calm, like we didn't just get kicked out of anywhere and he's used to being treated like a dirtbag.

But I'm not. I feel like throwing a thousand M-80s through the Burger King drive-thru window and watching the place go up in flames.

"Would you like fries with that?"

"Hell no, motherfucker. But here's a stick of TNT you can shove up your ass."

What's the big fucking deal, anyway? I mean, it's not like the place is crowded or we were causing any trouble. All we were doing was standing there.

So I tell that to Africa, but he just shrugs like he couldn't care less. I guess he's already too busy thinking about USA, where there's gonna be a thousand kids and he can grab tits and ass and pretend it's all an accident.

Then he goes over to pump gas for tips, and I just stand there and watch him run around like a fucking monkey for a couple of lousy nickels.

I don't know if it's getting my stuff stolen, getting kicked out of the Burger King, or watching Africa like that, but it all just gets me in a real sour mood. I don't know. Sometimes, I get all these weird thoughts in my head and I start thinking about what we'll all be like when we grow up. Take Africa and Fatty, for instance. Fatty's always running his mouth about being a porno star or a rapper when he grows up. It sounds stupid, but who knows? Maybe he'll do it. Maybe one day, we'll turn on the TV and Fatty'll be grinning at us from inside the screen and we'll all feel stupid for ever doubting his fat ass.

Either that or he'll end up some fat ajussy chopping off fish heads and cleaning out fish guts at his parent's store, bullshitting about how he makes two million dollars a year and going on and on about the good old days when he was a rapper, breakdancer, graffiti artist, playboy, and thug who had sex with a thousand women and beat up all these big black guys everywhere.

Still, I guess it's good that Fatty's at least actually got some ideas about his future, which is more than I can say for myself. I don't know what the hell's gonna happen to me when I grow up. Mom's always telling me to study hard, so I can be a doctor or lawyer or something high-class like that. But I don't wanna grow up to be no douchebag like Dr. Min or the lawyers who kicked Dad out of his store. Fuck it. Let the loser Korean kids at school do that shit.

Honestly, I don't care what I become or what I end up doing as a job as long as I don't ever have to set foot in no goddamn shoe repair shop or dry cleaner like my parents. Like I said earlier, I'd rather do anything, even rob banks or become a gangster like B.J., than work at some dingy little store with other ajussies next to me.

Still, as clueless as I am, I guess I'm still better off than Africa. It's not that he's lazy or anything like that. You already seen how he gets all worked up for nickels. But sometimes I just get this feeling that he's gonna grow up to be a squeegee guy or some guy who sucks tokens for a living or something super low like that. Like one time, I asked him what he wanted to be when he grew up and he gave me this look like he'd never even thought about stuff like that before. Not that you should be thinking about stuff like that all the time or anything, but with Africa, you just get that kind of feeling. Who knows, though? Maybe he'll surprise everyone and become some bigshot with tons of cash, a big house, and a fat limousine filled with naked girls, and me and Fatty will tell people how we used to play handball with him and how he was an ace in killers, rollers, and cuts.

Anyway, Fatty finally strolls out of the Burger King, holding a cup of soda and a half-eaten cheeseburger, even though he swore before that he didn't have a dime on him. The moment he sees me, he turns away and starts walking up Dongan back toward Broadway. The bastard's such a fucking baby sometimes. If it weren't for the fact that we all made a pact when we joined the Warriors, I'd ditch the kid, I swear.

I look over at Africa, who's busy pumping gas for some fat old geezer in a Cadillac, then take off after Fatty. It takes me forever to cross the street, so the bastard's got a good hundred yards on me. Anyone else with a lead like that would be impossible to catch, but Fatty's slower than shit.

Not that I'm fast. I won a race once when I was in fifth grade over all these other kids from all the schools in my district. But I hate running 'cuz it's boring as shit, which is why I didn't go out for the track team at school. The way I see it, that shouldn't be a big deal, but the track coach, this guy named Mr. Baker, who was also my gym teacher, took it as an insult like I was dissing him or something. So in gym, he had me race this black kid named Issac, who's the fastest kid on the track team, to show me up in front of everybody. I guess it might have worked. The only thing is, halfway through the race when we were still neck and neck, I just stopped running. Maybe Issac would have beat me. Maybe not. All I know is, I didn't feel like running just 'cuz some stupid dirtbag gym teacher told me to. Anyway, that drove the old bastard crazy. He started yelling at me in front of everyone for about half an hour about how running was the basic building block of everything and how I was a lazy good-for-nothing bum for not even trying to live up to my potential. I don't know about you, but potential or no potential, you gotta be a real dickless asshole to stand around and yell at some kid and tell him he's a bum just 'cuz he doesn't feel like running around for no reason.

Of course, even after all that, what am I doing? I'm running after goddamn Fatty in 100-degree heat up some godforsaken back road, where there's nothing except signs warning people that there's rat poison all over the place and a half dozen sketchy auto-glass places that look like they'd hire a kid like me in a second to go around and bust car windows to drum up business.

I finally catch up to the douchebag on the corner of Dongan and Broadway, right outside the Dan's Supreme, which is where Mom shops even though we live closer to the A&P.

"Why you gotta be a baby for? We were just playing around."

"Yeah, right."

"Come on, Fatty. It was just a joke. I swear. How the hell was I supposed to know you were gonna freak out like that?"

"Yeah? If it was just a joke, then why'd you push my hand and not Africa's? He was right there, too."

"How do I know? It just happened. But I didn't mean nothing bad. I swear."

"Just leave me alone, all right. You've been messing with me all day for no reason."

"What d'you mean, *all day?* I just pushed your hand into the dog. That's it."

"Yeah, right."

"Look, Fatty. You want me to say I'm sorry? I'm sorry."

He just stands there for a moment, then says, "Yo, that's a nice chain you got from Hindu Tim."

Goddamn! All the fuss about him being upset, and here he is sweating me for a fucking fake gold chain.

I take it off and and hand it to him. "Here. Take it."

"You sure you don't want it?"

I shake my head no. "You keep it. It fucking smells."

Fatty laughs a little, then puts the chain around his neck.

"Yo, how's it look, bro?"

"Good."

"Yeah? You think so?" He then goes to check out his reflection on a parked car window. And you should see him. I know I look in the mirror a lot, too, but the way Fatty looks at himself, you'd think he was some fucking movie star about to kiss his own damn reflection.

Anyway, he fixes the *Playboy* chain so that it's right in the middle of his chest, then starts rapping the Wikki Wikki song, *"Cuz when I was a little baby boy, my mama gave me a brand new toy. Two turntables with a mic, and I learned to rock like Dolymite. Time went by on this God creation. I knew someday I would rock the nation. So I made up my mind just what to do and I joined with the Fatty Production Crew."*

Then, just when he's up to, *"So go crazy, go crazy, don't let your body be lazy,"* he turns to me and says, "Yo, by the way, bro. You should have seen the shit I took back at Burger King. It was half diarrhea and had all these little green bits in it from all this spinach I ate last night."

"Damn, Fatty. How many times do I gotta tell you? I ain't interested in your dumps, man."

"But it was nasty. You should have seen it." He pauses. "Hey, what d'you say we go to the movies now? We can go sit in the air-conditioning and relax a little. Come on, bro. Like I said before, it won't cost you a cent."

Before I can answer him, Africa comes rushing up to us with Steven. I don't know why, but there's this huge smile on Africa's face, and Steven's smiling, too. It's like everyone looks so damn happy all of a sudden, like they ain't got a care in the world.

"You guys wouldn't believe what just happened. This old guy gave me a dollar just for pumping his gas!"

He sounds so goddamn happy and excited that Fatty and me just can't help laughing. I mean, I know a dollar's a dollar, but goddamn! Africa makes it sound like he hit the fucking lottery or something!

CHAPTER 20

I WOULDN'T HAVE believed it in a hundred years, but Fatty really does know the guy checking tickets. The only thing is, you could tell right away that the guy, this Spanish kid with a moustache, ain't too happy about Fatty bringing me, Africa, and Steven along.

Not that I blame the guy. Four freebies at two bucks a pop's eight bucks. If his manager ever found out, the guy'd get canned for sure and he wouldn't be able to dress up like a waiter no more.

Anyway, once we're inside, we go right past the concession stand, 'cuz everything there's a rip-off, and go to the very front of the balcony, where we can lean over the railing and see the people downstairs. It's the middle of the movie, but it ain't no big deal 'cuz we can always wait for the movie to start again and catch what we missed.

So we all sit there with these big smiles on our faces, waiting for the naked girls 'cuz God knows I could use a break from thinking about everything that's happened. And if the movie's even half as good as Fatty says it is, then it's gonna make my list of all-time best movies: *Getting It On*, *Porky's*, *Porky's II*, *Private Lessons*, *Losin' It*, *The Last American Virgin*, *Summer Lovers*, *Zapped*, *The Best Little Whorehouse in Texas*, and *Goin' All the Way*.

But the movie sucks. Thirty minutes in and there's not one fucking pair of tits. Instead, all there is is a couple girls in bikinis wiggling their butts every now and then, which is okay, but I could see that any day. All I have to do is hop the train to the five-cent pool in Astoria. It's like the people who made the movie are retarded or don't use their brains at all. I mean, if I ever made movies, you'd bet there'd be as many naked girls in 'em as you can possibly fit in one screen. Why have girls all dressed up when they can say the same lines just as good naked?

I tap Fatty's elbow with my elbow and say, "No wonder they let us in for free, Fatty. This movie sucks."

"Just wait a little, bro. It's gonna get good soon. You'll see."

We wait and wait, but the movie never gets better. So Africa and me, who're bored shitless, start checking out this couple who're making out in the very back of the balcony instead. They're going at it so hard and the guy's feeling her up so much it's like they're having sex except they still got their clothes on.

We go on staring for a long time, but they don't even notice us. Either that or they're getting off on having us look, like out of one of those letters from the magazines, where people always have sex in the subway or in some elevator.

Then, when the waste of film finally ends and the lights come on, all of us nearly faint 'cuz we finally see who the girl is. It's Hindu Tim's sister, and she looks hotter than ever, which's so fucked up 'cuz the guy's she's been making out with all through the movie is some Spanish homo with a bandana on his head like one of the guys from Menudo. That's the thing with girls who're real fine. I don't know why, but they always go for losers with bandanas.

I tap Fatty on the shoulder and say, "Ain't you gonna do nothing? Your girl's cheating on you, man."

Fatty turns bright red and says, "Leave me alone, bro," like he's all pissed and Hindu Tim's sister really is his girl and she really is cheating on him. What can you say? The kid really takes the cake.

We hurry out to the lobby. I look around to see if maybe Jin's there, but he's not. There's no girl giving blowjobs either. All there is is this beat-up photo booth that'll take your picture for a buck and a half dozen ratty video games.

Fatty goes over to the Defender game and pops in a 100-won Korean coin, which's worth like 10 cents.

I'm okay at video games, but Fatty's amazing. The son of a bitch couldn't catch or throw if his life depended on it, and he always finishes last whether we race on foot, roller skates, or bikes, but he's a whiz at video games and has the high on nearly every game in town.

So naturally, Fatty starts clearing screen after screen with just his first guy. Maybe some little kid might think that's cool, but me and Africa are bored out of our minds. So I pull Fatty by his shoulder and say, "Come on, Fatty. Let's get outta here."

"Wait up, bro. I'm about to beat the high."

"You can beat the high any day. Let's get outta here."

"That's true. I am good, ain't I?" he says, all proud of himself, which makes me regret what I just said.

Anyway, as soon as Fatty finally steps away from the game, some little kid appears out of nowhere to take his man. Of course, any other person would just let the little kid play, but Fatty turns around and says, "Get off the game!"

The kid just goes on blasting the fire button like he didn't hear Fatty at all.

So Fatty grabs the kid and yanks him off the machine. "It's still my game, and I never said you could play."

The kid gets it and steps back, then just watches helplessly as the ship gets blown away. It's pretty damn cheap, even for Fatty.

"You got a heart of gold, Fatty," I say.

"What?" he says, like he doesn't know what I'm talking about.

"You could've let the kid play."

"It's my quarter," he says, forgetting all of a sudden that he didn't even stick in a real quarter but some worthless Korean coin.

Anyway, as we head toward the exit, Fatty says, "Holy shit!"

It's amazing. It's just like in those stories where you meet your most-hated enemy on some narrow bridge, right before both guys fight it out to the death or when the Count of Monte Cristo reveals his identity to Caderousse as that evil bastard's lying there dying.

The little Spanish kid who got rejected by the rim and cursed Fatty out's standing on the other side of the glass door in front of the lobby, holding a huge bucket of popcorn.

"Thank you, God," says Fatty, then hurries after the kid.

I guess the little kid must be spacing out from the heat or from just coming out of the movie 'cuz he doesn't see Fatty come right up to him, which just goes to show you that all the speed in the world ain't gonna do you no good sometimes.

With one swoop, Fatty knocks the bucket of popcorn out of the kid's hands and sends popcorn all over the ground.

"What the hell!" says the kid.

Fatty grabs him by the collar and says, "I guess it's déjà vu, you little fuck. I told you I'd get you, didn't I?"

"Get off me."

Fatty snickers a little, then says, "Why should I?"

"'Cuz Diego's my cousin. And you're gonna get your ass kicked."

"You?" says Fatty. "You're Diego's cousin?"

"Yeah. So get off me."

Fatty turns to the rest of us and says, "Check it out, bro. This is Diego's cousin. He's the one who's gonna kick our ass."

It's so not like what we expected that we don't even laugh. Sure, I told you before that I wasn't scared at all, but I guess all of us have been a little worried about Diego's cousin 'cuz you never know.

"You owe me a popcorn, fatso," says the kid.

"What'd you say?"

It's weird. I don't know what's up with the kid, but it's like he ain't scared at all, which makes me wonder for half a second if maybe the kid's some kind of freak who can fight super good despite being so damn small. But that don't make no sense either 'cuz if he could fight like that he would've fought us already in the morning. So what the hell is going on?

"I said you owe me a popcorn, you fat fuck. And you better make sure it's a large," says the kid.

Fatty's face turns bright red. He then gets right in the kid's face and says, "Don't you get it, kid? I'm gonna kick your ass."

"You can't do shit to me, you fat fuck. My brother's here, and he's gonna kick your ass." The kid then points across the street with his chin.

We look over and see what we've all been quietly dreading the whole day. Out of all the kids who've ever mouthed off about getting backup, fucking Diego turns out to be the one kid who's for real. Diego's walking right toward us with the meanest, scariest kid we've ever seen. The kid's not even a kid, really. He's more like some six-foot thug with muscles like all he ever does is lift weights, which's the only real way to get cut up 'cuz that Charles Atlas stuff's just baloney. The thug sees us and smiles and I swear to God, the gold cap in his front tooth goes *ting!*

None of us has to say nothing. We all know there's only one thing for us to do. And we can only do it if we stick together and be brave. All for one and one for all, and all that. So that's what we do.

We all turn around and start booking.

From behind us, the little kid starts screaming, "Get 'em, yo! Especially that fat kid!"

CHAPTER 21

EVEN THOUGH DIEGO and his cousin are chasing us, we'd never think of riding the subway without paying and none of our parents have ever shoved us under the turnstile when the token clerk wasn't looking. So we get on line and wait like everyone else and purchase four tokens with money Fatty digs up from inside his socks. The token booth clerk tells us to be good boys and we tell him to have a nice day.

Yeah, right. Maybe on Pluto or Uranus, which is right next to your butthole and around the corner from your balls. Why the hell would we buy tokens when we can just jump the turnstile and hear the loser in the token booth shout, "Pay your fare!"?

Not that I know why they even bother. The guy might as well tell us to stop jerking off or getting hard-ons.

Anyway, as soon as we fight our way up the stairs, a smile appears on all our faces 'cuz there's a train right there in the platform with this huge *"NATO SABE"* piece on the side. The colors are all crazy like the guy's on drugs or something when he tags up, but it's so dope it should be up in some museum instead of all the crappy paintings of sunflowers they got there instead.

Not that we can exactly stand back and admire the piece right then. Diego may be slow as shit, but you can bet he'll be coming up the stairs anytime now.

So we bum rush the door, but it closes right in our faces. It's like the subway's dissing us and leaving us to get our asses whooped.

Fatty wedges his fingers into the rubber strip between the doors and tries to force them open, but it's a waste of time. He might as well try spinning the earth the other way to make time go backwards, which looked fake even in the damn movie.

"We're fucking dead," he says.

And I nod. 'Cuz our luck's finally run out on us. There's

nowhere to go, and in a few seconds Diego and his cousin will pop out of the stairs and start kicking our ass.

Like hell they will!

We're the Warriors and they're just a bunch of dumb spics. So I run over to the middle of the cars and yank the metal gate open. It's a lot easier than it sounds 'cuz it's made to come right out.

Then all of us jump on, even Steven, which just goes to show you the kid's not as soft as you'd think he is sometimes.

When I latch the gate back behind us and the train starts moving, the three amigos appear and start running alongside the edge of the platform like that'll actually do anything. We smile and give them the finger. Even Steven joins in the fun and sticks his tongue out at them. The little kid who cursed Fatty out tries to spit at us, but it doesn't even come close.

As we pull out of the station, Diego's cousin gives us the evil eye and runs his finger across his neck. Sure, it's a little scary. But we're out of there, so who the fuck cares? We know what he looks like now, so all we gotta do is keep our eyes out for the son of a bitch.

The train starts moving faster, and Fatty starts rapping real loud, *"I'm fat and fresh and super bow-leg-ged. From the thousands of girls that I've bed-ded. Upstairs and down, I'm big where it counts. I'll show you motherfuckers, it weighs 10 pounds."* He then folds his hands across his chest and says, "Yo, you like that, right?"

"Survey says," I pause. "Eeeeeeehn."

I know it ain't that funny, but we all crack up anyway 'cuz all of us are feeling good from making yet another getaway.

"Check it out, bro. No hands," says Fatty, holding his hands out to the side for half a second.

It's corny, but all of us do it, too. Believe it or not, it's actually fun. It's almost like we're surfing except there's no ocean, no waves, and we ain't got no surfboards.

"Hey, you guys hear that?" says Fatty.

We all look over at him. He's standing there with one hand cupped over his ear.

"What?" I say.

"That sound," says Fatty, tilting his head down to one side.

We quiet down and listen, but all we hear is the sound of the train, which is so loud that you gotta wonder how all the people in the buildings alongside the tracks ever get any fucking sleep.

"What the fuck you talking about, Fatty? All we hear's the train," I say.

Fatty shakes his head. "You guys gotta be kidding me. You gotta get your ears checked. Listen carefully, bro. You don't hear that?" He tilts his head even more to one side.

I look over at Africa, who just shrugs. He doesn't know what the hell Fatty's going on about either.

Then, just when we're all about to give up, Fatty rips one. It's less like a fart and more like an explosion. And instantly, the worst smell you can imagine, worse than 10 jars of rotting kimchi or 40 dead dogs, fills the air all around us. It's like he's set off a dozen stink bombs right inside our noses.

Steven cringes and fans the air in front of him. The kid's got a hard enough time breathing with his asthma, Fatty's fart's probably ripping huge holes right through the poor kid's lungs.

Fatty cracks up, then pulls up his T-shirt and slaps his belly. "If you guys want more, just let me know. I got me a lifetime supply in here."

Whoever delivered him must have been on drugs 'cuz he's the only Korean kid I know who's got himself a fat outie like the kids from Star Lake. And I think back to all the times at school when Fatty would tell everyone sitting around him to pass it on that he's about to cut one before ripping one or the tons of times he farted on purpose in gym while we were stretching just to make everyone crack up. The bastard's amazing. It's like he's this walking eating-shitting-farting-peeing-stealing machine that runs on cheeseburgers and twin pops.

Anyway, even though all of us are breathing in Fatty's deadly fumes, we all got smiles on our faces. Below us, all of Elmhurst is moving past in a blur. And like that, in a blur, the place doesn't look half bad.

Fatty then says, "Diego's cousin ain't all that, bro. I don't even know why we ran before. I could have taken that motherfucker."

"Yeah, right," I say. "That's why you ran up the stairs so damn fast."

"Real funny, bro. Tell you what. Next time we run into those suckers, I'll take care of Diego's cousin by myself. You and Africa take care of Diego and that little kid."

"Sure, Fatty," I say.

Fatty just shakes his head then slaps Africa in the back of the head. "What the fuck were you thinking anyway when you bet him, bro? You didn't really think that spic would pay up, did you?"

Africa doesn't say nothing.

"What did that spic bet you anyway? A bottle of Spic and Span?"

"He bet me *G.I. Joe*s numbers one and two."

I look right at him. "Say that again. What did Diego bet you?"

"*G.I. Joe*s numbers one and two."

A shiver runs down my back. It's the clue I've been looking for the whole day.

"Two fucking comic books for a pack of jumping jacks. Goddamn, that spic is stupid," says Fatty.

The guy doesn't get it. And he won't get it until I spell it out for him later. But for the first time all day, it finally feels like I'm actually getting somewhere.

CHAPTER 22

"SO WHAT'S THE VERDICT, bro? You see your shit anywhere?" says Fatty.

The bastard knows damn well we don't see shit. He just wants to hear me say I was wrong. But there's no way in hell I'm gonna tell him that. I know the super's guilty. He's just doing a good job of hiding it. Anyway, it ain't like we can even see all that clearly through the crusty window. Things would be different if we were actually inside the bastard's apartment. But from where we are, there's just no way to know for sure.

"I told you it'd be a waste of time to come up here, bro," says Fatty.

I don't say nothing. It ain't that I thought the super would have my stuff sitting out in the open right in the middle of his living room. I know the sorry douchebag couldn't be that stupid. But then again, who knows, right? After all, the guy was stupid enough to give my comic books to Diego a day after stealing them from me, so who knows what other stupid things he's done? But we don't see my stuff anywhere. Instead, all we see's a crummy living room with piles of newspapers here and there and old laundry draped over chairs and tables. It's not as bad as at my house, but it's pretty bad. But they're from the fucking jungle, so they probably don't know better.

I should know better, too. But I just can't leave so empty-handed. So I wedge my fingers under the window, which is open just a crack, and pull up.

"Yo, what the hell you doing?" says Fatty.

I go on pulling. The window finally gives and slides up half a foot, but the super's rigged it so it won't open any further.

"Damn, bro! What're you trying to do? Get us arrested?"

"Don't pee in your pants, Fatty. We ain't gonna do nothing."

It's true. I know better than to break in to some apartment, even if it's a crook's. Anyway, even if we wanted to go inside, the opening's not big enough for Fatty, Africa, or me to fit in. Maybe Steven could squeeze in, but having him do that would be crazy.

"Yo, let's get the fuck outta here already. I don't wanna get no J.D. card," says Fatty.

I give him this look 'cuz I can't believe that's what the fucking kid is scared of. Getting fucking J.D. cards. What can you say? The bastard's got the heart of a lion. Either that or he's used up all his guts fighting all those big black guys in Brooklyn.

Anyway, there's nothing more for me to do. It ain't like we can exactly have a cookout on the super's fire escape. So I slide the window back to the way it was, so the lazy fuck won't catch on that anyone was spying on him. Then we get the fuck out of there.

When we're back on the ground, Fatty says, "Admit it, bro. You were wrong about the super."

There's actually a smile on the bastard's face. It's like the kid wants me not to find my stuff.

"We don't know that for sure. The super might have it hidden somewhere," I say.

"Sure, bro. And the Mets could win the fucking World Series."

I just stare at him for a while. After all that bullshit about how he's got my back and all that, here he is bitching and moaning like it's so fucking hard for him to help me out a little. I swear, I know we're all part of the Warriors, but the kid's worse than Diego sometimes.

Anyway, I ain't in the mood to argue with Fatty. So I start walking back around to the front of the Holland. The only thing I can do now is hope we run into Jin and that he saw something.

I don't know. Maybe it's just me getting my hopes up for nothing like I've been doing the whole day, but more and more, I just get this weird feeling that Jin knows something, and everything will make sense once I talk to him.

Of course, just as we're about to go into our building, Fatty says, "We're wasting our time, bro."

I turn to him and say, "I gotta talk to Jin. He might have seen something."

Fatty rolls his eyes like he so doesn't wanna be there with me. "What?" I say.

"Nothing."

"Don't give me that. Why the hell'd you roll your eyes at me for?"

"Fine. If you really want to know, it's 'cuz I think it's kind of laughable that you're still going on about looking for your shit."

"What's so 'laughable' about it?"

"Yo, I'll admit that looking for your shit sounded kind of fun this morning, bro. And even looking through the super's window just now wasn't that bad. 'Cuz it was all like we were playing detective. But it's getting stupid now. I mean, if it were that easy to figure out crimes, every crook in the world would be behind bars. I know you think you're all smart and shit 'cuz you can do the Rubik's Cube and all that. But give me a fucking break. What makes you think you can find out who ripped you off when even 5-0 couldn't do nothing?"

"That's 'cuz they didn't even try."

"Maybe it's 'cuz they knew it'd be a waste of time."

"Damn, Fatty. What's your fucking problem? You're the one who thought it was the super in the first place. You're really gonna tell me that Diego having those comic books ain't suspicious to you?"

"No, Pete. It ain't suspicious at all. So what that dumb fuck has comics? I got comics, too. You gonna tell me now that I broke into your apartment and stole your shit just 'cuz I got a couple of *G.I. Joe*s?"

"That's different and you know it. You've always had comics. Diego didn't have them before."

"So what? Maybe that dumbass started collecting 'em. Or maybe he was just running his mouth. It don't prove shit. You said it yourself. It ain't even like the super has a master key."

"This ain't about no stupid master key."

"Just 'cuz Diego has a couple of comic books don't mean the super ripped you off. Just think about it, bro. If the super's some crazy thief like you say he is, then why the hell does he drive around in that fucking wreck? If he's a thief, he'd be driving around in some souped-up Cadillac, not some busted old wreck."

"Maybe he does that as a disguise. Anyway, the super's not all poor. Just look at Diego. He's got brand new Adidas all the time. How the hell does the super afford Adidas for Diego? You tell me that."

"How the hell do I know? Maybe he collects cans. Ask that bastard if you're so damn curious."

I stand there glaring at Fatty, wondering why he's gotta be such a fucking asshole.

Fatty turns to Africa and says, "Yo, don't just leave me hanging like this. What d'you think, you bowl-headed motherfucker? You don't really think the super did it either, do you?"

Africa's quiet for a while, then says, "I'm not sure."

"What d'you mean you're not sure?" I say.

He looks at his feet, then says, "I'm not sure, Pete."

"What the hell's that supposed to mean?"

"I'm not sure that Diego really has those comic books."

"What d'you mean you're not sure? You said that's what he bet you, didn't you? Did he bet you those comics or not?"

He doesn't say nothing.

"Damn, Africa! It's a simple question. Did Diego bet you or not?"

"He did."

"So what the hell are you talking about, then?"

"That's just it, Pete. He said he had them. But he never actually showed them to me or anything. He could've just been bull-shitting me, for all I know."

I let out a groan.

"See that, bro? Africa knows what I'm talking about," says Fatty.

"This is crazy. I can't believe you guys are actually taking the super's side."

"We're not taking nobody's side, bro," says Fatty. "We're just saying you need some more proof. Some real e-vi-dence."

"The super already takes stuff from us. And Diego has comics he never had before. What more proof do you need?"

"How about maybe someone who actually saw the super breaking into your apartment or carrying your shit out the building? How about something like that, bro?" says Fatty.

"I told you. Jin might have seen something. That's why we're going to talk to him."

"Give me a break, bro. If Jin saw something like that, he would have come to you already."

"Jin might be looking for us right now."

Fatty rolls his eyes again. "Yeah, sure. He's looking for us so hard that we ain't seen him the whole day. Trust me, bro. Jin's got problems of his own."

"Fuck you, Fatty."

"Don't get mad at me, bro. I'm just telling you what's what. All I'm saying is, let's just say everything's the way you say it is and the super's some crazy crook who's got everybody fooled. Then why don't you go to 5-0 right now and tell them to arrest him? Come on, bro. I dare you. All you gotta do is go over to a pay-phone. You ain't even gotta pay no money. So go ahead. Tell the cops about Diego's comic books. Let's see whether they come arrest the super or not."

I never thought Fatty would be able to shut me up in an argument, at least when we're arguing about something important and not about whether Bruce Lee was killed by ninjas or not, but I just can't let Fatty shut me up like that, and it's not just 'cuz of the stubborn gene I got from Mom and Dad, either. The bastard's a retard for fucking crying out loud. And even though I don't get good grades in school, I know I gotta be at least 50 times smarter than the dumb fuck.

But for some reason, I can't come up with nothing smart to say, so I just shout, "I ain't going to no fucking cops, all right!"

"Of course not. 'Cuz you know you ain't got no real proof and they'll just laugh in your face."

"That ain't it, Fatty. Only fucking jerkoffs go to cops. All cops do is shove donuts down their fat face and scratch their ass. I can take care of this on my own!"

"What are you gonna do, bro? Go ask the super nicely if he took your shit and hope he'll say yes? Or maybe you think you can tackle him from behind like you did Diego and beat it out of him? What's it gonna be, bro?"

I don't know why Fatty's being the way he is, but it pisses me off so much that I almost want to punch him in the face. One good shot is all it'd take to bash in his bowling-ball head and knock some fucking sense into the son of a bitch.

"You know what I think?" I finally say.

Fatty and Africa just stare at me.

"I think you're both chickenshit! Just like this morning when the super took your ball, Fatty. And just like when Diego shoved you, Africa. You guys just stood there and didn't do shit 'cuz you were scared. It's the same thing right now. You're so damn scared of the super that you think nothing's going on, when all the proof is staring us right in the face."

Fatty shakes his head. "That's bullshit, bro. And you know it. I ain't scared of the super. Hell, I ain't scared of nobody. That motherfucker might be bigger than me, but I'll fuck him up. I'll knock his ass out. But that don't change the fact that you ain't got nothing on the super and you know it."

I shut my eyes for a moment and take a deep breath. "Fine, Fatty. I get you now. After I stuck up for your sorry ass this morning to try to get your football back and after I backed you up all those times at school when the other kids call you a freaking cow, you're just gonna leave me hanging."

"It ain't like that, bro."

"I thought we were friends, Fatty. I thought we were all the Warriors."

"We are."

"You sure? You're always going on about how you got my back. But I guess all that's just talk, huh? It's like everything else that comes out your mouth. None of it means shit."

"Damn, bro. Why you gotta put words in my mouth for?"

"I ain't putting nothing in your mouth, Fatty. But it's okay. If you don't wanna help, then don't! I don't need your damn help. But I'll tell you this much. If it was your apartment that got robbed, I'd be right there helping out, doing whatever until you got your shit back. You can bet on that."

Fatty looks down at his Pumas, then says, "I'm sorry they stole your shit, bro. But I just can't get in any more trouble this summer, bro. I'm already in deep shit for getting left back."

He says "left back" like it's some disease that he got 'cuz of bad luck and not 'cuz he cut so many classes and never did no homework.

"You should see how my mom rags on me now. I'm telling you, bro. If I do anything wrong now, my mom will kill me. I'm not kidding, bro. She'll pack my shit and send me to go live with my aunt in Jersey. Where they live, there's nothing there but cows."

"Your mom ain't gonna do shit."

"Trust me, bro. She will. She's mad as hell right now. It's all because of that freaking bitch, Ms. Waters. She could have passed me, but she didn't 'cuz she hates my guts. God, if I knew where she lived, I'd throw a brick right through her window. Anyway, let's just forget the whole thing. What d'you say, bro? Let's go to USA. I'll even lend you some money."

Steven starts pulling my arm for some reason, but I'm too busy being pissed off at Fatty.

"Do whatever the fuck you want, Fatty!"

Steven tugs my arm again. The kid can be so damn annoying like that. So I turn to him and he points to the door of the lobby where Hindu Tim is running out in that retarded slow run of his.

Hindu Tim sees us and stops dead in his tracks. And for a second, it looks like the kid might start running again and it'll be déjà vu all over again like how Fatty's always going on and on about. But the kid doesn't run.

"What the fuck you want, Shitstain?" says Fatty.

Hindu Tim walks right past him like he ain't even there and comes straight to me.

"What's up, Tim?" I say.

"I just saw Jin go home. You can see for yourself that I wasn't lying before."

The kid sounds so damn serious like it really was killing him that we thought he was lying. You'd figure a kid like him wouldn't give a fuck what we thought of him on account of how we mess with him all the time. But it's exactly the opposite. It's like he cares so damn much.

"Goddamn, you fuck. You're still bugging us about that shit?" says Fatty.

"I wasn't lying before. He's got bruises. And I know who gave them to him."

"Yeah? Who? Gandhi?" says Fatty.

"His brother B.J."

Fatty stares at the kid for a second, then slaps him hard right across the face. Hindu Tim's skin's almost black and way darker than Africa's, but the slap's so hard we can still make out the print from Fatty's hand.

"What the hell, man?" says Hindu Tim, in this super whiny voice he has whenever someone hits him.

"I told you before not to fucking lie to us."

"I'm not lying."

"You are and you know it. Now get the fuck outta here before I kick your ass again."

The way Hindu Tim glares at Fatty, for a second, I almost expect to see the kid finally fighting back. But then the kid just chickens out like always and reminds us again just how tough he is by starting to cry.

I don't know about you, but seeing the tears flow out of his eyes makes us all feel this incredible sense of guilt. We should know better than to mess with him just because we can. That's what a kid crying can do for you. It can make you realize that what you did maybe wasn't right. And there's no point in picking on someone just 'cuz they're a little different from you, and everyone would be so much happier if we just all learned to be kind to one another, even to kids like Hindu Tim, who's just misunderstood and only wants other kids to like him for who he is.

Yeah, right.

It ain't like we've never seen Hindu Tim crying before. And all it does is make us wanna mess with him more 'cuz there's nothing I can't stand worse than crybabies. So all of us just stand there and rub our eyes and make like we're crying, too.

Hindu Tim shakes his head, then starts walking away up the street. Big fucking deal he can breakdance. He can grow up to be the best breakdancer in the world, he'll still be a fucking doormat 'cuz of how soft he is.

Fatty picks up an empty soda can lying in the gutter and

chucks it at the kid. It just misses him, but still manages to make him jump, which of course just makes us crack up even more.

Then Fatty turns to me and says, "You believe that fucking Hindu, trying to tell us B.J.'s back?"

"Maybe he's telling the truth."

"Trust me, bro. If Jin's face's busted up, he got jumped or his dad fucked him up. But it wasn't no B.J."

Something about the way he says that gets me all curious. So I look right at him and say, "How d'you know?"

"Trust me, bro. I just know."

"How?"

"I can't tell you, bro. But I know. So let's just leave it at that."

"Spill it, Fatty," I half shout.

He sighs, then says, "Fine. But you forced it out of me. And you gotta swear you won't tell nobody. 'Cuz I know I ain't too good at keeping secrets, but this is different. This is real messed up."

"Fine, Fatty. Now tell us."

"Jin's mom came to my house two weeks ago to talk to my mom. I knew something was up 'cuz my mom had me stay in my room. But I stood right by the door and heard everything. She told my mom how B.J. might come back sometime next month, but she wasn't sure of the exact date 'cuz that's up to the judge."

"Why's he need a judge to come back from Korea?" I say.

"That's the crazy part, bro. B.J. ain't in Korea. He was never there. It's all bullshit. His parents just said that to hide the fact that his ass was locked up in jail all this time."

"Jail?"

"Yeah, bro. Jail, where they try to buttfuck you and shit. He got locked up 'cuz he blew some guy's brains out right in some restaurant in Flushing. Bam! Execution-style. It's all 'cuz he joined a Chinese gang, bro. Fucking chinks make us Koreans do all the dirty work."

I just stand there for a while. 'Cuz if what Fatty's saying is true, then Jin and his family are all fucking liars and Fatty's actually managed to keep a secret for two fucking weeks.

But there are things in Fatty's story that don't make sense, so

I say, "If he blew some guy's brains out, how come he got out so quick? He's only been gone for a year now."

"That's the part I'm not too sure about. But he's gotta go to court again. If you ask me, he probably snitched and cut some kind of deal like in the movies. Anyway, you guys gotta promise not to tell nobody. And don't say nothing to Jin. You gotta promise me right now. Not one word to Jin, all right?"

Me and Africa nod. It's weird. Usually, we'd think that anything Fatty says is bullshit. But for some reason, we believe him this time. I guess the truth is, none of us actually really bought the story about B.J. going back to Korea to serve in the army. If you really stopped to think about it, that never made much sense at all. But then again, if what Fatty said is true, then B.J., who's only like 19, is a fucking murderer, like one of those guys in the movies or one of those guys that gets written up in the *Daily News*, which is crazy 'cuz as tough as B.J. is, none of us ever thought he'd actually ever kill anybody. I mean, how do you go from fighting black kids in the street to killing some old guy in a couple of months?

"I don't know, bro," says Fatty. "I know it's messed up and all that to knock on someone who's down, but I'd be glad if that sucker never got outta jail. I've been all patient all this time 'cuz he's Jin's brother. But one of these days, me and that punk is bound to knock heads and I'm gonna have no choice but to kick his ass. Anyway, don't tell nobody about this, all right? And don't say nothing to Jin."

Me and Africa nod again. Then we all duck into the lobby. The only thing is, as soon as we step inside, a hand shoots out of nowhere and grabs me by the shoulder.

"Get off me!" I shout, and try to free myself.

But it's no use.

I don't know what it is about dickheads like the super and that ajussy from the V&B, but they all got hands like vises.

"You were on the roof today, throwing firecrackers," says the asshole.

"I don't know what you're talking about!" I may be just a kid, but even I know that whenever someone accuses you of something, the best thing to do is deny it and pretend you don't know nothing.

"Don't lie to me, boy. I saw you. You and your friends. All of you are in big trouble."

"I told you, I don't know what you're talking about. I wasn't on no roof."

"Don't lie to me, boy! You threw firecrackers at me and my car! Then you pissed at me. You pissed at me!"

He gets right in my face and starts shaking me. "You think you can get away with that?"

"Go to hell!"

The fucker's eyes flash with anger. "You don't talk to me like that. You hear me, boy! You don't ever talk to me like that!"

"Fuck you, asshole! I can talk to you whatever way I want. You're just a fucking janitor!"

He lifts his other hand like he's about to slap me. But I don't flinch. I know the douchebag ain't got the guts to hit a kid, at least not in the middle of the fucking lobby with three witnesses looking right at him. But even if he did, I don't give a fuck. He can hit me all he wants. He's a fucking crook and cursing him out feels fucking great.

The bastard just stares at me for a long while. Then, just when it looks like he's gonna chicken out and put his hand down, he pulls himself together and slaps me hard right across the face. The slap's so loud it echoes off the walls.

Some other kid might back down then, but I don't. I've been slapped before. Sure, it hurts, but it don't kill you, so fuck it.

I stare right at the super and say, "Fuck you, asshole."

He starts shaking and goes apeshit, slapping me again and again. A fucking grown man beating up some little kid right in broad daylight.

It's not even the actual slaps that hurt, but the fact that I'm getting knocked around by some brainless dickhead who doesn't deserve to live and there's nothing I can do. I swear, it fucking sucks being a kid sometimes.

When the bastard finally stops slapping me and lets go of me with a shove, he just stands there for a while, catching his breath, then says, "Tell your parents about this, and I'll tell them what you did on the roof."

Then he goes out the door and I turn to Fatty, Africa, and Steven, who're all just standing there with these weird looks on their faces.

"Yo, you all right?" says Fatty.

"It's nothing. It didn't even hurt," I say. Of course, that's not true. The entire left side of my face feels like it's burning.

"Yo, tell your parents and have them sue his ass, bro. Have his ass locked up for child abuse."

Fucking Fatty and his bright ideas. He just stood there the whole time and watched the super kick my ass. But now that the super's gone, he's got a thousand and one fucking ideas.

But what good will telling my parents do? They would never believe me. And even if they did and had the money, they would never hire no fucking lawyer, not after how the Jew landlord and his lawyers stole Dad's store from him. Not that I give a fuck. Lawyers are even more worthless than cops and supers. I can take care of my own problems.

So I turn to Steven and say, "Go up the stairs and wait for me outside Jin's apartment.

He nods, then does exactly what I told him.

"Yo, what're you gonna do?" says Fatty.

I don't say nothing. I just go over to the elevator and press the button for it to come down. The super might have slapped me around, but that don't mean I'm scared of him or that I don't see right through him. I know exactly why he hit me. It ain't 'cuz of no fireworks or me being up on the roof. The bastard knows I'm on to him, and he's just trying to scare me. But I ain't scared. 'Cuz I know he's a thief. And I ain't gonna let him get away with it. Hell no!

CHAPTER 23

T HE ELEVATOR CREAKS like some stray cat that's being tortured. It's like everything else in the building, all busted up and no good. At this rate, the whole place will be condemned in a couple of years and a wrecking crew will come tear the place down the way they did the empty warehouse before they put up the Green House. When that happens, no one will even know we lived there once. Which is why we gotta leave our mark now. Not that that's what we're doing, but within seconds, the puddle on the floor gets so big that we all have to move out of the way so that we don't step in our own pee. Of course, we can't help but step on it a little bit and we're all breathing the steam coming up from the stuff. But at least we got our shoes on.

Sure, it's gross. And sure, as dumb as the super is, he's bound to put two and two together and know it was us. But who the fuck cares?

The bastard's still gonna have to mop it up 'cuz every person who takes the elevator will be pounding on his door, moaning and groaning until next week if he doesn't. It's like the time the boiler kept breaking last winter. Everyone in the building, including all these old ladies you woulda never thought would complain about anything, stood outside the super's door and screamed all these curses you woulda never thought no old lady would scream, which just goes to show you how pissed people will get if you take away their heat and hot water.

Anyway, the elevator comes to a stop all of a sudden. So we zip up our flies and get ready to play dumb.

Then the door opens, and there's Mr. Schnell with his empty shopping cart. I guess the guy can tell right away that something's not right, but when he actually sees the steaming puddle, his face changes and he gets this horrified look like he just saw the most disgusting thing in the world, which just makes you wonder.

Here's a guy who saw everyone in his family get killed in a concentration camp, where they put people in ovens, and he can't take a little pee in the elevator floor. I just don't get it.

Anyway, if it had been anyone else, maybe I'd do something wise like hold my nose with one hand and fan the air with the other and say, "I guess the super couldn't hold it." But I just can't do shit like that with Mr. Schnell. Maybe it's 'cuz the old guy's looking right at me with this pained look on his face like I let him down somehow, but it's like my tongue's stuck all of a sudden, which really sucks 'cuz bullshitting my way out of jams is one of the few things that I'm really good at.

A couple of seconds later, Mr. Schnell shuts the door, and the elevator starts moving again.

It's all for the best, I guess. This way, at least Mr. Schnell will know that I ain't no different than any other kid in the Holland, no matter how many books he gives me. And he'll finally stop talking to me about how everything's getting messed up everywhere because of the *schvartzes*.

CHAPTER 24

JIN'S FLOOR'S JUST like everyone else's. The hallway ain't seen a mop in months and the one fluorescent bulb's flickering on and off like it's about to go out any second. When it does, you can bet the super will take weeks to replace it 'cuz he's too damn cheap to shell out for a new one.

Steven's waiting for us exactly where I told him to, which is one good thing about the kid. I don't know if he can tell what we just did, but he just stares at us for a while.

"He didn't go out, did he?" I ask.

Steven shakes his head no.

So I ring Jin's bell and knock on the door, but there's no answer. I press my ear against the door, but there's nothing. No TV, no radio. No nothing. It's like I'm back on my paper route, trying to collect from the deadbeats looking to stiff me. All I know is I ain't gonna give up. Like everyone in my family, I can be pretty damn stubborn when I want to be.

So I keep ringing Jin's doorbell and banging on his door. "Come on, Jin. It's me. Open the door! We know you're in there. Hindu Tim saw you."

After the hundredth bang, there are footsteps on the other side, then a soft voice.

"What d'you want?"

It's Jin.

"Open the door, Jin. I gotta talk to you!"

"I can't."

"What d'you mean, you can't?"

"I just can't."

"Open the door already, you freaking retard!" shouts Fatty.

I shoot him a look to let him know to shut up. He just shrugs like he ain't got a clue that he's annoying the shit out of me. The guy didn't even want to help me look for Jin. Now, he's gotta make like he's all gung-ho about it.

I turn back to the door. "Come on, Jin. We just want to talk to you."

"You shouldn't be here."

"Open the door, Jin. Please."

There's a clicking sound from Jin's lock. Then his door creaks open a couple of inches, and Jin peers out through the space between the chain and the door. Even through that tiny space, we can see right away that his face is all busted up.

"What happened to your face?" I say.

"It's nothing. I fell," he mumbles, looking down at the floor. He's never been a good liar, and it's so obvious he's not telling us the truth.

I guess Fatty thinks the same thing 'cuz he says, "Yo, what happened for real? Your dad go nuts on you or something?"

Jin shoots him a dirty look, then says, "My dad didn't touch me."

"What's the big fucking deal? If your dad hit you, he hit you. You don't gotta try to hide it."

"I told you, it wasn't my dad."

The way he says it only makes it seem like it was him even more.

"Fine. Then who was it?" says Fatty.

Jin doesn't say nothing. I guess the guy's embarrassed that his dad beat him up, but that's always how it is with kids like that. Their dads will beat the shit out of 'em for no reason, and they'll still try to defend their loser dads like that's gonna change anyone's mind.

Now, I ain't gonna try to tell you that no parents should ever hit their kid, but you gotta wonder why parents are always taking shit out on their kids. Not that I know a whole lot about it 'cuz besides Mom, who loses it every once in a long while and goes nuts on me, Dad's never laid a hand on me. That's the thing with Dad. Even though he tries to act all strict sometimes and used to be a teacher back in Korea, which is how he and Mom met, when it comes right down to it, he's a complete softy, which is why everyone says I'm spoiled and have an attitude problem and why

Mom thinks I get into trouble all the time. Maybe they're right. But the way I see it, whatever I do wrong, if my own father ain't gonna go off on me, what right does anybody else have to yell at me for?

Anyway, I gotta find out about the super, so I look right at Jin and say, "Listen, Jin. I gotta talk to you about something."

He looks up. And I tell him about the robbery and ask him if he saw the super.

But he just shakes his head and says, "Sorry, Pete. But I didn't see anything."

"Are you sure?"

"I didn't see the super. But you should go talk to Roman."

"Roman?"

"Yeah. He was hanging around outside the building."

I wanna kick myself in the head so bad. I've been running around in circles all day. And now I gotta go talk to the guy who hates my guts more than anyone alive.

"You guys better go," says Jin.

Fatty shakes his head and says, "Not so fast, bro. Where's my fucking money?"

Jin shoots Fatty a dirty look, then says, "You'll get it. Just not today."

"You better pay me, bro. I'm not playing around. I told you what I was gonna do, right?"

"Yeah, Jin. You better pay him, bro," a hoarse voice calls out to us from the stairwell.

It's like hearing the voice of a ghost. We all stop breathing for a moment, then turn around slowly to see if it really is who it sounds like.

And there he is, leaning against the wall just outside the stairwell, back from the dead like Jason at Crystal Lake. Who knows if he's coming back from Korea or jail, but it doesn't even make no difference. 'Cuz just like that, Jin's bruises, his going m.i.a. on us, everything makes perfect sense. It's like Jin just told us. His dad didn't lay a hand on him.

B.J. smiles at us and takes a drag from the cigarette that's dangling from his mouth. Then he says, "Have you kids done it yet?

If you haven't, let me know. 'Cuz I know a good girl. A real pro. Trust me. Your first time's always better with a pro."

At least, that's what he should say. Then we'd all laugh and kid around and go have a beer.

Instead, he just says, "I had to take the stairs up. Seven fucking flights 'cuz some wiseasses peed in the elevator. But I'm sure you kids wouldn't know anything about that, right?"

None of us says anything.

B.J. walks past us and says, "Don't just stand out here, guys. Come inside. Have some sandwiches."

Fatty nudges me with his elbow.

I look up at B.J and say, "It's okay. We were just leaving."

B.J. shakes his head. "No, no. I insist. Make yourselves at home. It's been a while since I saw you kids. I wanna know what you've been up to."

Fatty shoots me a look. So does Africa. I don't know what they expect me to do. It ain't like I can do anything. We can't get over by making like we don't speak English, and B.J. couldn't care less about Kato or any stairs. We can't even make a run for it, 'cuz B.J. would just chase us down and make us suffer even more.

So I step inside. The others follow me reluctantly. It's like we're walking the plank and B.J.'s about to feed us to the sharks.

CHAPTER 25

I KNOW NOW ain't exactly the time to be thinking about stuff like this. But I can't help thinking maybe I wouldn't be out looking for my stuff like some fucking idiot on a scavenger hunt and we all wouldn't be lined up against the wall in B.J.'s living room, waiting for B.J. to torture us, if Dad hadn't lost $10,000 that one time. Then I wouldn't have had to do my paper route and I wouldn't give a fuck about no goddamn Atari.

I take that back.

'Cuz Dad didn't exactly lose that money. It's more that he gave it away 'cuz he wanted to be some bigshot in front of Mom's old church. He stood up in the middle of Sunday service and promised to give the church $10,000 on account of the minister making a special announcement the week before about how Dad's store was doing so well that he had to hire a worker.

Believe it or not, his store did do pretty well for a while back in the day, at least good enough that he'd always come home all smiling even though he was covered in grime and had to take a bath as soon as he stepped into the house. I guess that's what having a bundle of cash coming in every day does for you.

Anyway, things were so busy that he had to hire this guy named Hernan Cortes—I swear to God that was his name—to do a lot of the work for him. The only thing was, Hernan was Colombian, so naturally, he was an alcoholic and a drug addict and would disappear every now and then for days at a time without a fucking word.

Hernan would also show up at our door in the middle of the night sometimes, completely wasted with bloodshot eyes, and start crying about what a good, kind man Dad was. Anybody could see he was just carrying on like that so he could get his hands on a couple of bucks. But Dad would always fall for it.

Anyway, you should have seen what a fuss the minister and

the other people at that church made 'cuz of Dad's announcement. All these people kept coming up to me afterwards for weeks and telling me how lucky I was to have such a generous man for a father and how God would bless us and all that. The only problem was that Dad didn't have the $10,000 yet, and then his store started doing bad 'cuz who the hell's gonna get their shoes fixed for five bucks when you can get a pair of Fayva's for ten? Dad's always going on and on about how the shoes at Fayva are garbage 'cuz they ain't made right, but I guess no one else seems to care.

But a promise is a promise, especially when you make it in front of a hundred greedy ajussies and ajoomas. So the minister and everyone at church kept hounding Dad to pay up, and Dad did, even though it took a while and he had to work his ass off. If you ask me, it was stupid. But that's the kind of guy he is. Stupid.

Anyway, as soon as Dad finished giving the church the last of the money, we switched churches. So basically, it ain't that I don't believe in God, but after going through that circus act, I swear, I'll never give another penny to any church for as long as I live.

Maybe you might think that's not Christianlike of me. But I don't give a fuck. Take now, for instance. What the hell's God or Jesus gonna do for me, when B.J. has all of us lined up against the wall?

B.J. stares at us for a long time without doing or saying anything. Then, after what seems like forever, he starts pacing in front of us and says, "It's beautiful out. You kids should be out playing. But instead, I come home to find you crawling around here like a bunch of fucking cockroaches. Does that seem right to you? Does that seem like the kind of welcome I deserve?"

None of us says nothing. It's so quiet we can hear the refrigerator humming all the way from the kitchen. Either that or they got one fucking noisy fridge.

B.J. shakes his head and turns to Jin. "Roll up your sleeves."

Jin just stands there.

"I said, roll up your sleeves!"

Jin does, but real slow.

B.J. then takes his cigarette and holds the burning tip right over the kid's forearm and makes like he's gonna burn him with it.

He then turns to the rest of us and says, "So what's it gonna be? Any of you guys want to take my brother's place? How 'bout it, guys? We got any heroes in here?"

None of us says nothing.

He gets right in my face and says, "How 'bout you? You want to be a true friend and take his place? You wanna give me your arm instead?"

I don't say nothing either. As much as I wish I were brave enough to take Jin's place for him, I can't. I ain't tough like that. So I just look down at the floor and shake my head.

"See that, Jin. When it comes right down to it, not one of your so-called friends is willing to go to bat for you. Remember that. That's how life is. So don't go around thinking you got friends or that you kids are tough. I've seen tough guys, and you kids ain't tough. Being tough isn't about fighting a couple of niggers. So listen to your moms and do like they say. 'Cuz you don't ever want to end up like me, all right!"

He then shoves the tip of the cigarette right in Jin's arm. Jin cringes, but doesn't let out a sound, not even when there's smoke coming from his skin and you know there's gonna be a scar there forever.

Standing there and watching B.J. torture Jin like that, I can't help feeling so damn small 'cuz B.J.'s right and we're all fucking cowards. Then, just when it seems like the nightmare just might end, B.J. says, "Now, all of you do me a favor and let's go for a walk."

The way he says it, so calm and quiet, almost makes it seem like we have a choice. But we don't. 'Cuz you just can't say no to a guy who might very well be a fucking killer.

CHAPTER 26

THE ELEVATOR RIDE down takes forever, and Fatty, Africa, and me never look down or at one another. We all just keep our heads up and our eyes glued on a different part of the wall.

A piece of paper in front of me says the elevator's safe for up to 12 people, which is a joke 'cuz it's almost packed with just the three of us.

Fatty and Africa get off on their floor without saying nothing. I don't say nothing either. B.J.'s the one they should be pissed off at, but they act like it's all my fault, the fucking cowards.

The elevator stops again and I get out on my floor. My socks are soaked through and a trail of cold pee follows me to my door.

I go inside and chuck my socks in the garbage. Then I go to the bathroom and start washing my feet in the tub. The hot water's dead, but the cold water gushes out like there's no tomorrow.

I scrub hard with this red Korean wash towel that feels like sandpaper. It's what Dad used to use to get the dirt off as soon as he came home when he still had his store.

After my skin turns all red, I dry my feet and walk out to the living room, where Steven's waiting for me with Jin. I didn't even hear them come in. It's like they're ghosts or fucking ninjas. Jin's even dressed like one. He's got on this hooded sweatshirt, I guess to hide his arm and the bruises on his face.

With anyone else, I might be embarrassed by how messy our apartment is. But it's only Jin, so I don't give a fuck. No matter how crummy the place is, at least no one's giving me cigarette burns and beating me up for no reason.

I climb up the boxes that fill one entire wall almost to the ceiling and fish inside the top box for a pair of sneakers that fits me. There are sneakers of every size. So no matter how big my feet get, there'll always be a pair of fake Puma's for me.

While I'm lacing up a pair my size, Jin comes over and just stands next to me without saying nothing.

"What, Jin?" I say. I know that B.J. messing with us ain't Jin's fault, but I can't help taking it out on him anyway. He should have opened the door quicker instead of being such a pussy about it. Then we would have been out of there before B.J. ever showed up.

Jin looks down at the floor and mumbles, "I'm sorry, Pete. I don't know why my brother's the way he is."

I didn't ask him for no explanation. I feel like going off on him and telling him how I know all about how his brother was in jail and not in Korea all this time and how his family's nothing but liars and murderers. But he sounds so damn sorry and his face is such a mess, I can't help feeling bad for the guy. So I just stand there and say nothing.

"I'm sorry, Pete. If I could kill him, I would. I really would. I wish he was dead," he says.

There's such a weird look in his eyes. They're blank, as if he isn't even looking at me. It's like he's about to break down and start talking to himself like those teachers at school who can't take it no more and have nervous breakdowns.

Just then, a cockroach the size of a quarter crawls across the floor like it couldn't care less that we're standing there. So I reach down and smack it dead with my shoe.

It's the five thousandth roach that I've flattened, but they always keep coming back. It's all 'cuz of the fucking super. Instead of bringing a real exterminator, the bastard tries to do it himself and always does the crummiest job.

CHAPTER 27

FATTY'S STANDING UNDER the powerline in his fucking flip-flops. All he needs is a toothpick and a paper fan, and he'd look just like the loser ajussies hanging out at the park with my dad.

All our sneakers are hanging 20 feet above us. Of course, mine are the only no-names there. Even Africa, who runs around like a monkey for five lousy cents and nearly cums in his pants for a crummy dollar, had himself a pair of Ponys.

Fatty picks up a rock and hurls it at the sneakers, I guess to try to knock them loose. But he's got himself a fucking lollypop arm. So he misses wide by 10 feet, and only manages to scare the three pigeons that are sitting on the powerline. The dumb fucks fly around in a big circle, then return to the exact same spot. A thousand watts of electricity are running through them, but they don't seem bothered at all.

"Shit!" Fatty mutters, then flings another rock.

"Forget it, Fatty," I say. "There's no way you're gonna get them down."

"My mom's gonna kill me, bro. She bought me those Pumas just last week. She's gonna fucking kill me. Those sneakers cost 30 bucks."

"Damn, Fatty! Will you stop with your shoes already?"

"Go to hell, bro. Maybe you're not worried about your sneakers 'cuz they're some cheap three-dollar shits your dad couldn't sell. But my sneakers cost real money!"

"Shut up, Fatty," says Africa.

"No, bro. It's about time I started saying what's up." He then looks right at me and says, "None of this would have happened if we weren't going around looking for your stupid Atari. I know the super's stupid, but even he's gotta know better than to break into your apartment, bro. The only thing worth anything in there was your fucking Atari. Everything else was junk. Everyone knows you sleep on beds your dad picked up out of the garbage. Shit! You don't even have a fucking air conditioner."

"Shut up, Fatty," says Africa.

"It's all true, and everyone knows it. That's why you and your brother went to that welfare camp for niggers and only wear hand-me-downs. I don't even know why we went along on this stupid goose chase. It was a fucking waste of time. Your Atari's gone, bro. I don't know who ripped you off. But whoever did it got away with it. And there's no way in hell you're ever gonna get it back! So stop wasting your time already."

I smile as cool as can be, like his words have no effect on me whatsoever. "That's not true, Fatty. The super has it. I just haven't figured out where."

Fatty rolls his eyes. "Keep dreaming, bro. The super doesn't have shit."

"I ain't dreaming. I'd explain it all to you, but you wouldn't be able to understand even if I told you. That's why you got left back and that's why you're gonna be in special ed with all the other retards learning how to use a spoon."

Fatty tries to play it off cool, but I know he's pissed. Any moron who's been left back and headed to special ed has to know he's stupid and hate it. He tightens his lips and stays quiet for a while. I can tell he's trying to think of something cool to say, but it's not going well. Finally, he blurts out, "Yeah, well at least my dad isn't a fucking loser who couldn't even shine shoes for a living!"

There's just silence for a moment.

Then Fatty says, "Your dad's a loser, bro. Only losers clean shit off other people's shoes. And your dad couldn't even do that right. Why do you think my dad never invites your dad over to play cards? Africa's dad comes over all the time. He and my dad both think your dad's a bigtime loser." He turns to Africa. "Tell him, bro. You were there the other night. You heard them."

Africa doesn't say nothing.

Fatty says, "Face it, bro. Your dad's a fucking loser! And you know it, too. That's why you lied to Ms. Gold that your dad owned a sneaker store when everyone knows he shined shoes by the subway station."

It's not that I disagree with the bastard or that I'm defending my dad's honor. I'm not. I ain't no goddamn sucker in some kung-fu movie. I couldn't care less about my dad or what Fatty thinks about anything. But I can't just have the fat bastard mouth off to me like that, especially in front of other kids. I started the Warriors. And I'm the fucking leader. And anyway, I've been wanting to wipe the stupid fucking grin off Fatty's face for a while now.

So, *THWACK!*

I catch the bastard right in his nose, which is easy 'cuz Fatty's face is just about as big a target as there is.

To my surprise, Fatty manages to fight back a little and actually takes a couple of swings. I guess the kid's been practicing real hard at Tiger Chung Lee's. But like I've been saying, tae kwon do's garbage, so the fat fuck can do forms for the next 20 years and it wouldn't make no difference. I'm faster and tougher. And I don't close my eyes when I punch. So the whole thing's over in less than a minute. The bastard never had a chance.

After getting hit a dozen times, the douchebag stumbles over his own feet and falls to the ground. Some other kid would wait for the fatass to get back up on his feet, but I don't. I pounce on the kid and kick him right in the stomach again and again until he crunches up like some goddamn fetus and starts yelping.

When it's all over, Africa, Jin, and Steven rush over to us. But this fight ain't nothing like my fight with Diego. No one pats my shoulders. No one touches my back. Everyone just stands there like they can't believe what just happened.

Fatty gets up slowly and glares at me.

He and I've had fights before, but none of them were like this. All the other times, I'd just put him in a headlock and it'd be over. But not this time. No one says nothing. And no one tries to get us to shake hands. I doubt Fatty would even take my hand if I offered it, which I would never do, and I know I sure as hell wouldn't if he did.

Finally, Fatty says, "You think you're so tough, bro. How come you didn't do nothing against B.J.? How come you didn't do nothing?"

'Cuz B.J.'s scary, and Fatty's a tub of lard who should keep his big mouth shut. But I don't say that. I don't say nothing. I just turn around and start walking up the block. Fuck the Warriors. So all of us grew up together. Big fucking deal. It don't mean shit. If Diego would have been born Korean, he would have been a Warrior, too, and you already seen what a dick he is.

Steven rushes over and walks with me. For the first time all day, I'm actually a little glad the kid's with me.

From behind us, Fatty shouts, "At least my dick's not all cut up like some fucking freak's! Fuck you, Stitch!"

I don't say nothing. The bastard can say whatever he wants. Everyone just saw how I kicked his fucking ass. But Steven turns around and gives the bastard the finger. Good for him, I think to myself.

Fatty shouts, "Go to hell, you little freak!"

Steven holds up his middle finger even higher. The kid's impressing me more and more. Maybe the kid does have guts. Maybe there's hope for him yet.

CHAPTER 28

I SWEAR TO GOD I have no idea what the fuck Fatty's talking about. My dick's perfectly normal. So all the kids who ever called me Stitch can all go fuck themselves.

Sure!

I'm sure you believe that after all I've told you so far. Truth is, it's a fucking miracle that I can still pee out of my dick considering how this welfare f.o.b. doctor chopped off a good chunk of it last summer. And if you think I'm exaggerating, you can go fuck yourself.

It all happened 'cuz my brilliant fucking dad read in the Korean newspaper how not being circumcised was bad for you and could lead to problems later on. So he sent me to Dr. Min.

Of course, the first thing the stupid son-of-a-bitch doctor does is have me take my pants off, so he can look at my dick. I don't know what it is about doctors, but they always wanna look at your dick.

Anyway, when he's done checking my dick for God-knows-what, he looks me right in the eye with this dead serious look in his eyes and starts asking me all these stupid questions in his ajussy English, like if I had sex all the time 'cuz my dick was all purple and bruised up. I don't know if it's just me, but having some washed-up 50-year-old ajussy loser look at your dick and ask you about your nonexistent sex life just doesn't make you feel all that hot.

So, naturally, I shouted, "No, you brainless dickhead! I haven't had sex yet. My dick's purple 'cuz I jerk off all the time, all right!"

You should have seen the look on his face when I said that.

I wish I could have seen it, too, 'cuz I never said it.

Instead, I just kept quiet and played dumb and hoped the bastard wouldn't rat me out to my parents 'cuz the last thing I need is to have my mom grill me about why I'm jerking off all the time.

Of course, as big a brainless douchebag as Dr. Min was, a part of me kind of felt bad for the guy. I mean, here's a guy who probably studied like a maniac and probably never missed a single homework or a day of school in his entire fucking life. And all he's got to show for himself is some shithole of an office next to the bus station and some titless dog-faced shriveled-up wife for a receptionist. And what's he got to look forward to all day? Cutting up little kids' dicks and sewing 'em up again.

Anyway, when Dr. Min was done snip-snipping and stitching me up, the real fun began 'cuz then I had to walk home. The first five blocks wasn't so bad since my dick was still numb from the shot I got before the operation. But the last five blocks took me two hours and felt like someone was holding a torch to my dick. Then, for the next two weeks, I had to sit around naked with a paper cup taped over my dick and wash off all the blood every six hours with cotton balls, so that the stitches wouldn't get infected. All that pain and aggravation 'cuz Mom and Dad didn't think to have the doctor cut me when I was born.

I guess things might have been different if I was born in the U.S. and not in some shithole of a country. That's another thing I forgot to tell you about. I was born in South Korea, which honestly, I don't feel too hot about. How can you feel hot about a place where half the people are fucking ajussies and all the kids grow up to be such fucking goody-goodys? Not that I had anything to do with it. The way I see it, I could have been born anywhere. What counts is that I wised up fast, which's a good thing 'cuz at least I know how to take care of myself.

Take today for example. What the fuck would have happened if I was some goody-goody dumb fuck? I've had two fights—four, if you count the V&B guy and the super slapping me around. Diego and his cousin are after me. B.J.'s back from who knows where. The Warriors are history. And it ain't even 4 o'clock yet.

Still, a part of me can't help thinking maybe Fatty's right. Maybe there really is something wrong with my dad. Fatty's parents weren't kicked out by their landlords. Neither were Africa's. So why did it happen to my dad? And why did he get so crazy about the stupid sunflower painting that time, and why the hell does he sit around his ass at the park instead of getting himself a job? It's not even like he drinks a lot or does drugs. And I know he's not lazy 'cuz he used to work hard.

All I know is that things are fucked up. Which is why Mom's worried all the time about how me and Steven are getting messed up. She's always going on, for instance, about how me and Steven don't have good manners and how every single photo we have is ruined 'cuz Steven or me is sticking out our middle fingers. She's got a point. But we only do that for fun. It ain't got nothing to do with manners. Of course, what really gets Mom worked up is how I'm always going over to other kids' houses, but never bringing no kids over to ours. She's always telling me how I shouldn't be ashamed of our apartment or about who I am and all that, which is all good and easy for her to say. But she's not the one who's gotta listen to Fatty go on and on about how your dad picks up mattresses from the garbage.

All of a sudden, Steven turns to me and says, "Fatty's a fucking dick."

I just stare at him for a while. I'm almost proud of him. It's the smartest thing he's said the whole day.

So I mess up his hair and say, "Don't listen to anything Fatty said, all right? He's fucking retarded."

Steven nods. His eyes are red and he looks like he's about to cry, but I don't get mad at him. The kid's just little. That's all.

"I told you I'd get you back."

The voice is right behind me, and I want to kick myself so bad. There's no way anyone should be able to sneak up on me like that, which just means I don't know how it happened, but something's definitely wrong with me.

I turn around, and there's Diego, staring at me with the biggest grin I've ever seen on him. I guess I'd be grinning too if I was in his shoes and standing there with his two cousins.

"I told you I'd get you back, didn't I?" he says.

"But Kato's in the stairs," I say.

"What?"

"Kato's in the stairs," I say again, but my luck's run out on me a long time ago, and I ain't got no more tricks left.

"Yo, what the fuck's he talking about?" says Diego's little cousin.

"I'm not sure. I think he's talking about Bruce Lee," says Diego. He then gets right up in my face and says "You didn't think you could run forever, did you?"

It's clear now that I'm not gonna be able to talk my way out of this. So I do my last trick, which I save only for the biggest and most desperate emergencies. I spit on his face.

He wipes the spit away and says, "You're so dead, man!"

"Fuck you."

Diego's big cousin, who's been quiet all that time, steps right up to me and says, "So you're the fucking chink who thinks he's a tough guy, huh?"

The guy looks even more vicious than before. And he's got the type of face I wish I had. One look and you know he's not someone you should mess with.

All of a sudden, Steven shouts, "Why don't you just leave us alone?"

The thug turns to him and says, in a whiny high-pitched voice, *"Why don't you just leave us alone?"* Then he says, back in his natural voice, "Why the hell should I? 'Cuz you're gonna start crying if I don't?"

Diego starts cracking up.

"Leave him alone!" I shout.

The thug turns to me and says, "Why? 'Cuz you're gonna make me?"

"I just might."

The bastard looks like he's about to explode. He glares at me, then turns back to Steven. He then turns to the little kid from the Colony and says, "Yo, Orlando, you and this little kid are about the same size. You think you can take him?"

The little kid takes one look at Steven and nods.

The thug turns back to me and says, "I'm gonna do you a favor, punk. I don't know why, but I feel kind of generous today. So instead of kicking your ass personally, I'm gonna have my little brother fight your little brother. A fair fight. One-on-one. No one's gonna jump in. Then everything will be squashed."

I look over at Steven. He's got this look on his face like he's about to have another asthma attack. Maybe that'd make Diego and his cousin feel sorry for us and leave us alone. Yeah, right! Things are so bad, I'm lying to myself. The only thing is, I can't even lie good no more.

The little Spanish kid goes over to Steven and shoves him hard in the chest. Steven just stands there like some retard.

The kid shoves him again, and Steven still doesn't do nothing. It's like he learned how to fight from Africa.

"You fucking bastards. None of you has the guts to fight me one-on-one!" I shout.

Diego and his cousins all turn to me.

"Come on! I'll take all three of you on!" It ain't that I'm crazy or trying to be a hero. Far from it. It's that I know Diego's cousin's gonna fuck me up anyway, even after Steven gets his ass kicked, so why make the kid go through all that?

Diego's cousin smiles at me. I swing right for his chin, but it's no use. The guy ain't some punk you can catch with a sucker punch. He calmly steps out of the way, then starts beating me silly, landing one solid punch after another.

The whole thing ends in less than 10 seconds. I'm no match for the guy. A punch catches me right in my chin, and all I see is a flash of white.

The next thing I know, I'm flat on my back staring at the sky, which is just one big stretch of blue. And for a short while, I forget where I am and why I'm lying there. It's just me and the sky. Normally, I should be up on my feet, pumping my fists in the air and pretending I won even though it's clear to everyone else that I got my ass kicked. But I just don't feel like it. What'd be the point? Fucking B.J.'s right. I ain't no tough guy. So who the hell am I kidding?

The only thing I do wanna do is ask Diego about his comic books, but the words never come out of me. I guess I know it'd be a waste of time. The douchebag wouldn't tell me shit.

Then I hear Diego shout, "Yo, chill, man!"

I look up and see Diego's cousin, right up in my face, holding a knife.

"What the hell you doing, man?" says Diego, grabbing his cousin's arm.

Diego's cousin shakes Diego's hand off and yanks me up by my hair.

I don't even move. There's no use. Why fight it when fighting won't do no good?

CHAPTER 29

I FLING A BOTTLE at the train. It clangs off and lands in the
bushes somewhere.

I can barely see out my right eye. Diego's cousin got me
exactly where Diego got me. I don't know how bad it looks, but I
know it's gonna look a hell of a lot worse tomorrow. And I don't
even wanna see what my hair looks like. But I can imagine.

"Come on, Pete. Let's go home," says Jin.

I don't know how he found me, but there he is in his sweats,
holding Steven's hand while the kid's bawling like the stupid little
kid he is.

"I'm staying right here. You can go if you want!" I shout.

Steven starts to cry even more, but I just don't care anymore.
He can cry all day if he wants.

I can't explain why, but I can't stand the sight of the kid all of
a sudden.

So I turn to him and start shouting, "I'm sick of looking at
you, Steven. You hear me! You give me the creeps, you know
that! What's wrong with you? What the hell do you got to cry
about?"

"I'm sorry, Peter," he says.

I don't know why the hell he's saying sorry or why he's such a
goddamn crybaby. But it only makes me madder.

"What the hell's wrong with you, anyway? Always tagging
along and making me look bad. Why'd you just stand there when
that kid hit you? How many times have I told you you don't let
anyone just hit you? What the hell's wrong with you?"

"I'm sorry, Peter."

"Get the hell outta here. I'm sick of looking at you. Go on
home and leave me alone. Go on. Get outta here!"

Steven starts walking away.

Jin stares after him, then turns to look at me like he expects me to do something. Fuck him. So what if I'm not the best big brother in the world? At least I don't burn the kid with cigarettes like B.J. does to Jin, right?

I pick up another bottle and fling it high in the sky. When it comes down, it clangs off a tree branch and falls in the bushes. But it doesn't break. It's like everything I do's a fucking dud.

CHAPTER 30

NIGHT TAKES FOREVER to come, but when it does, it comes quick, and everything goes from gray to black in seconds. Then me and Jin are there by ourselves, sitting in the dark in front of a small fire like two bums. All we're missing is a couple of tin cans and some sorry stray dog licking at some old bone by our feet.

Every now and then, a train goes by and blue sparks fly out from the tracks. Each time, I scream my head off. "Fuck! Fuck! Fuck!" I'm not even mad about Diego and his cousin. All I can think about is the super and how he's getting away with everything.

I don't know why, but I look up at the sky like some dumb kid, half expecting to see the Big Dipper. But there's not a single star. Like I told you before, I got me the dumbass touch. Everything around me turns into a dud.

For some reason, I start thinking about Roman, and not just 'cuz he's the only guy left that I haven't talked to about the robbery. But no matter how I try to justify what I did, I know I owe him an apology. I fucked up. There's no two ways about it. But then, what d'you say to a guy who knows that you peeped on his mom in the shower for two weeks? I know it sounds retarded, but that's exactly what I did. I broke their bathroom window by accident. And when the super didn't fix it for weeks and weeks, I started going out my window and climbing down to his fire escape every night to look in while Roman's mom was in the shower.

I did it night after night until Roman caught on somehow and ambushed me on the fire escape. You should have seen the look on his face when he saw it was me. I thought for sure that he was gonna clock me, but he just stood there without saying nothing, and I got the hell out of there.

I know how stupid all that sounds, and if I had it to do again, maybe I'da been smarter and wouldn't have done it. But then again, Roman's mom is hotter than even Hindu Tim's sister and you don't know how many times I've jerked off picturing her and me doing it. I know all this must sound pretty perverted, but like I told you before, that's my problem. I'm all sick like that.

"You hungry, Pete?"

Jin's voice startles me, and I look up at him.

"You hungry, Pete?" he asks again.

I shake my head no, but my stomach growls real loud. Some fucking summer. Even my own stomach's dissing me now. Next thing you know, I won't be able to control nothing and my head will start spinning around like in *The Exorcist*.

Jin laughs a little, then says, "It'd be good if we had some TV dinners."

I nod.

TV dinners *would* be good. Fatty would swipe them from the A&P, and we'd cook them up in the fire like we were camping. Of course, they'd never come out right 'cuz they're supposed to be cooked in ovens. They'd get all burned on the outside, especially the apple pie part, but they'd still taste damn good.

"Sometimes I stay out here all night," says Jin. "I bet you guys didn't know that, did you?"

I didn't, but I'm not surprised. Jin's probably got the most fucked-up family out of all of us.

He takes out a small metal flask and takes a swig. Then, when he notices me staring, he holds it up to me and says, "It's rum. It'll help you sleep good."

I take a swig, and hand the flask back to him. He puts it on the ground by his feet and says, "You ever think of running away, Pete?"

It's a weird question. But Jin's a weird kid, so what d'you expect?

"Not really," I say, even though it ain't true. Sure, I've thought about running away. Who hasn't? But I ain't gonna just come out and say that.

But Jin does. He says, "I think about it all the time. Sometimes, I wanna get out of here so bad. But I can never figure out where the hell to go."

That's the thing with hanging out with Jin. He'll always tell you the most goddamn depressing things. I mean, things that are guaranteed to make you wish you weren't even alive sometimes, which just makes you wish you were hanging out instead with even some stupid idiot like Fatty. 'Cuz as stupid as Fatty is, at least that bastard will make you laugh once in a while. With Jin, the kid can cut a fart and it'll come out sounding sad and depressed.

The fire dies down a little and I throw in a broken chair leg to keep it going. Then I turn to Jin and say, "Can I ask you something?"

"What?"

"Why did your brother beat you up so bad?"

He doesn't say nothing, and I regret that I ever asked him.

So I say, "I didn't mean nothing by it. Forget I asked."

"It's all right. I don't know why. He just did."

That don't make much sense at all, but I nod anyway. From somewhere nearby, we hear bottle rockets and M-80s going off. Fourth of July is still a few days away, but everyone's been setting off fireworks since a month ago.

"How come you didn't tell anyone your brother was back?" I don't know why I ask that. But I guess I wanna know.

Jin just shrugs it off like it's no big deal, like I asked him why he drinks Pepsi instead of Coke.

"Fatty says he was in jail and not in Korea all this time. Is that true?"

He just shrugs again, and it's clear that what Fatty said is all true.

"You think he stole your stuff, don't you?" he says.

"I never said that."

"You don't have to. I would think it, too, if I were you. But you're wrong. He didn't do it 'cuz I was with him the whole day."

I don't say nothing. I just throw another broken chair leg into the fire. I guess he's right. Still, if it weren't for the super, B.J. would definitely be my number-one suspect. 'Cuz it'd just be too much of a fucking coincidence that my apartment got robbed so soon after B.J. came back. And anyway, who else could have done it?

For some weird reason, I remember Mr. Schnell's book, which

is still in my goddamn pocket. I feel so stupid for carrying it around all day. So I take it out and chuck it into the fire. Whoever the Great Gatsby is, he can go to hell for all I care.

"Why'd you do that for?" says Jin.

I don't say nothing.

"You could have probably given that book to Roman. He'd probably have read it."

I stare at him. I don't know if it's the fire, but he's a dead ringer for his brother, which just makes you wonder how the kid lives with himself, 'cuz good-looking or not, every time he looks in the mirror, he must see his fucking brother staring right back at him.

CHAPTER 31

ROMAN'S BATHROOM WINDOW'S still busted. I don't know what time it is, but I guess it's almost 10 'cuz I can hear Mr. Schnell playing his fucking scales. You figure the old guy would get tired of playing the same thing over and over, but there he is night after night like some goddamn robot.

I keep tapping the window. I'll do it all night if I have to 'cuz I ain't got nothing else left to do.

The light in his room finally turns on and Roman comes over to the window and opens it. He's got on a Def Leppard T-shirt like he's trying to be some metalhead all of a sudden. I can't help feeling a little bad for the guy 'cuz he doesn't know what the hell he is or should be.

"I figured you'd come by," he says.

At least the guy's talking to me.

He then looks at my face and says, "Fatty said you got fucked up, but damn."

I don't say nothing. Knowing Fatty, he probably went around and told everybody how he kicked my ass.

"Look, Roman. I'm sorry about everything. It was stupid of me. I should have never done what I did. And I should have apologized sooner. I'm sorry."

He just gives me this look, then starts grinning. "So this is your apology, huh?"

"I'm serious, Roman. I'm sorry."

He grins even more. "So I guess you're gonna ask me now if I saw the super break into your apartment, right? Fatty told me all about it. I'm surprised you don't think it was me who robbed you."

"No, Roman. I don't."

"It ain't no big deal. It's all right if you do."

"I don't. I thought maybe you might have seen something. Jin said you were outside the building. But I swear, I didn't think it was you."

"I told you, I don't care if you do. To tell you the truth, I'm surprised everyone doesn't already think it was me."

"Did you see anything?"

"Yeah, I saw something. I know who did it. I saw them go up and down this very fire escape. I saw it with my own eyes."

"Who'd you see?"

He just smiles.

"Who, man? Who did you see?" I say again.

But he just goes on grinning.

"I'm not kidding around, Roman. Tell me who you saw."

"Go to hell, man. I ain't telling you shit."

"Look, Roman. I'm sorry about what I did. It was stupid. But don't hold that against me now. Please, man. I'm begging you."

"Yeah, yeah. You can say you're sorry and all that, but it ain't gonna change the fact I ain't gonna tell you shit."

"Come on, Roman. Tell me who it was."

"Fuck you."

"I told you I was sorry."

"Big fucking deal. So you're sorry. So what? What does that change?"

"What d'you want me to do, Roman? I shouldn't have done it. I'm sorry."

"You know something? I'm glad you got robbed. It couldn't have happened to a better person. 'Cuz you're a fucking asshole. You fucking stabbed me in the back, you know that? If it had been anyone else, maybe I would have understood. But *you*. I can't believe how stupid this sounds right now, but I used to think you and me were like brothers."

"We *are* like brothers."

"You should hear yourself right now. You're an even bigger bullshit artist than Fatty."

"I'm not lying. Come on, Roman. Let's just forget about all that. Please, man. I'm begging you."

"You say all that shit now. But you're just like everyone else. To you, I ain't nothing but a fucking nigger."

I just stare at him for a while. I have no idea what the hell he's talking about. I've never called him a nigger, at least not when he's been around. And I was always joking around like how me and Fatty call each other fucking chinks. I never meant it.

"It ain't like that, Roman."

"Sure it is. You can pretend now and act like we're cool, but you guys always had it in for me 'cuz I'm black."

"What the fuck are you talking about?"

"You know exactly what I'm talking about. You fucked me over 'cuz I'm black."

"You're only half black. And anyway, none of us cares."

"Yeah, right. That's why you fucking peeped on my mom."

"Look, Roman. I'm sorry I did what I did. But you gotta know it wasn't 'cuz you're black. I swear to God. I don't even know why I did it. I'm just all perverted, man. But it wasn't 'cuz you're black."

"Fuck you, man. Fuck you and all you Korean motherfuckers. You know, my mom would always tell me to be careful with you guys and not trust you guys a hundred percent 'cuz of how you guys were gonna turn on me someday 'cuz I'm black. But I never thought it was gonna happen. I thought she was just being fucking paranoid like she always is 'cuz of what happened to her and my dad. But she was right. She was fucking right."

I don't say nothing. Maybe Roman's right. Maybe I do hate black people even though I always go on and on about Star Lake and all that. I don't know what to think anymore. Everything's so fucking crazy.

Roman lights up a cigarette without even offering me one and says, "The funny thing is, I used to think hanging out with you guys was the best. I know how stupid that seems now, but I really used to think that. But it's all bullshit, isn't it? Ten years from now, you'll probably be in college or something like that, and I'll be stuck here pumping gas."

"It ain't gonna be like that, Roman."

"Sure it is. I ain't stupid, man. I know how things are. You fucking Korean bastards are gonna all grow up to have your own stores and niggers like me are gonna be working at Burger King 'cuz everything's all fucked up like that."

"What're you talking about? You really think you're gonna be worse off than Fatty?"

"All I know is I ain't telling you shit. And I don't care if you call the cops on me."

"Damn, Roman. What the fuck is wrong with you? I never said it was you."

"I don't care if you said it or just thought it. I don't give a fuck what you think, man. Just leave me the fuck alone, all right? So I saw who robbed your apartment? Big fucking deal. It ain't like anyone's even gonna believe me or you're gonna be able to get your stuff back. Anyway, I ain't saying shit to you, so what the fuck do you care?"

"It was the super, right?"

"Go to hell. And get the fuck out of my fire escape."

"Tell me, Roman."

"Fuck you. You can beg from now 'til forever, I ain't never gonna tell you shit. 'Cuz I don't know you. And you don't know me. So get the fuck outta here and have a good life."

He then goes back inside and shuts the window. And I'm left standing there, alone on the fire escape, wondering how it is that every single friend I ever had hates my guts now.

CHAPTER 32

THE SUPER'S CAR'S just sitting there under the streetlamp, daring me to do something, begging me to do something. I think about keying it, writing a nice message to cheer up the super tomorrow morning. But the super deserves so much worse.

So I pick up some pebbles off the ground. Then I fling them, as hard as I can, one by one, at the four side windows. That's the thing with breaking car windows. You'd think you'd need a brick or something, but one tiny little pebble's all it takes.

I finish all four windows in less than 30 seconds. There's no alarm so it's a piece of cake. No one even thinks to look out their windows. No one gives a shit.

I reach inside and pop the trunk, praying that my stuff will be there. But there's nothing there except an old blanket and a pair of old boots. Even Fatty's football's not there anymore, which just means the son of a bitch is smarter than he looks and is still one step ahead of me.

When I step away from the car, a voice calls out to me from up the block.

"Peter! Is that you?"

I freeze up. It's Dad. The guy doesn't have a job, but he's always coming home late. Who knows what the hell he does all night? It ain't even like he drinks.

"Peter!" Dad calls out again, hurrying toward me.

For a moment, I think about taking off. But I can't get myself to run. It's like my legs have a mind of their own. I just stand there and wait.

Dad comes up to me and sees the super's car with the busted-out windows, and just stands there for a moment without saying anything.

He then says, "Minho, look me in the eyes."

I do. And I tense up a little 'cuz I know how messed up I must look with all my bruises and my hair all fucked up like that.

He puts a hand on my face and says, "What happened to you today?"

"Nothing."

He makes that *tsk, tsk* sound again, then says, "I know you don't think much of me, Minho. And I can't exactly say I blame you. But I understand how it is to be a boy your age. I used to get into fights, too. But you don't want to grow up to be a thug." He then points at the car and says, "Tell me the truth. Did you do this? I don't care if you did or not. What matters is that you're honest with me."

I can tell he's trying so hard to figure out whether I'm telling the truth or not. I guess he thinks he's an expert when it comes to stuff like that just 'cuz he was a teacher once. Maybe back then with other people's kids, he could tell if a kid was lying, but there's no way he can with me. I ain't nowheres as good a liar as Fatty, but I ain't no stupid kid who starts shifting or looking down at his feet when he says something that ain't true.

So I look Dad right in the eye and say, "I didn't do it. The car was like that when I got here. I was just looking around."

"You're sure?"

"I swear."

I guess he decides I'm innocent 'cuz he just nods. Then he flicks his cigarette into the ground and stubs it out with his shoe.

From off in the distance, another round of bottle rockets and M-80s goes off.

Dad clears his throat, then says, "You running around like this is okay with me, Minho. Boys will be boys. But your mother doesn't understand. It upsets her. And you gotta think about that. She works all day. She deserves better. You understand, don't you?"

I just stare at him.

He smiles and starts walking back toward the Holland. I follow about six feet behind him, without a word, like that guy in that movie after the nuns squeal on him.

It's weird. I got over on the guy again, but I still feel crummy. It'd be so much better if the guy was just a drunk who slapped me around all the time. At least, then I wouldn't feel so bad about hating his guts so much.

CHAPTER 33

I WAKE UP the next morning with a puddle of sweat under me and my hand wrapped around my dick. I don't know what's wrong with me. After the day I had, you'd figure my perverted dreams would take a time-out. But they just come on even stronger. Who knows? Maybe I'm an even bigger pervert than Fatty.

I put on a beat-up Mets cap to cover my new haircut, and go outside with Steven. The street's empty. There's no sign of Fatty, Africa, or Jin anywhere. They're probably off somewheres making a new crew with Fatty as the leader. Knowing the dumb fuck, he'll name it the New Warriors or Warriors II.

The super's bananamobile's still parked in the same spot, except the busted windows have been taped up with plastic bags. The super's so cheap, he'll probably drive around like that for years.

I know the super's gonna come after me. But I'll deny everything and make like I had nothing to do with it. No one saw me. So fuck it. It's just like him robbing my apartment. He ain't got no proof, so what the fuck is he gonna do?

While I'm standing there, the lobby door swings open and the super and Diego come outside. They're both carrying fishing poles and large plastic buckets.

I tense up and ready myself for the super to go off on me. But he just glares at me for a while, then goes to his crappy car without saying nothing.

Diego starts following his dad, but I grab his arm and say, "Yo, I gotta talk to you."

He looks like he doesn't know what to do, but then he nods, and me and him walk off a little ways down toward the corner.

"I'm sorry about your hair," he says. "But it was all Freddie's doing. He's not even my real cousin. He's just some guy I know. I didn't know he was gonna flip out like that. I swear, man."

"Forget it."

He looks at me funny for a little bit, breathes a sigh of relief, then says, "Thanks."

"But I want to ask you about the comic books you bet Africa."

"What about them?" he says, all defensive all of a sudden.

"Do you really have them?"

"What d'you mean?"

"I need to know if you really have those comic books. *G.I. Joe*s numbers one and two." I stare right at him. I can usually tell whether someone is lying or not.

"What for?"

"Look, just tell me if you have 'em and where you got 'em from."

"Why? 'Cuz you think my dad stole them from you?"

I don't say nothing.

"Fatty told me all about it. I just have to say you're crazy."

"Look, just tell me yes or no. Did you get the comics from your dad?"

"Go to hell, man! My dad didn't steal nothing. I bought those comics myself." He pauses. "I know you guys all think my dad's a big loser. And I know you guys hate my guts, but you got no right to mess with him! And don't think my dad don't know what you did. He knows it was you who broke his windows. I don't know why, but you're just lucky he's not calling the cops."

He's almost crying now. And I don't know what to make of it. All that time, I figured he didn't give a shit about his dad like the rest of us kids in the building about ours.

"I'll tell you one thing," he says. "At least my dad's got a job. You don't see him bumming around the park all day."

"Fuck you, you spic. Your dad's a crook. And I'm gonna prove it."

He shakes his head and goes over to his dad.

I stare after him. I guess it's good that he looks up to his dad and all that and is even willing to lie for him, but how he feels about his dad doesn't mean shit. Lots of kids think their parents are good. And tons of mothers think their children are angels. But that don't mean shit. Shit, I'll bet even B.J.'s mom used to think he was an angel, too. All I know is, the super may have everyone fooled, even his son, but he can't fool me. Hell no!

CHAPTER 34

I TURN TO STEVEN, who's got this scared look on his face. And for a moment, I think about just forgetting the whole thing. I could always go back to folding newspapers at the Optimo and sweeping the sidewalk outside the A&P. Big fucking deal the manager's a faggot and a child molester. If he tries to grab my dick, I'll fucking knock his ass out.

But I just can't.

So much has happened, and I've come too far to turn back. It's like the old fisherman in that book. He might not have brought the fish back, but he stuck it out, which I used to think was fucking stupid, but I don't anymore.

So I crouch down in front of Steven and say, "Steven, I need you to go inside that window and open the door for me."

He looks at the window and turns back to me and starts shaking his head no.

"Please, Steven. I never asked you for anything before. I always take you wherever I go and stick up for you when the other kids tell me to ditch you. And I fought that crazy guy so that you wouldn't have to fight the other kid. I'm asking for just one little thing, Steven. Do this one thing for me. Please. You're the only one who can squeeze through."

He doesn't say nothing.

But I don't let up. I put both hands firmly on Steven's shoulders and look right at him. "Please, Steven. This is the only way. No one believes me and there's nothing else I can do. I wouldn't even ask you if there was another way."

The kid just stares at me. I'm so close to losing it. I shut my eyes and take a deep breath. When I open them, Steven's looking right at me. Tears are welling up in his eyes. He looks so afraid and so damn pathetic.

But I don't care. I have to get inside the super's apartment. I hold up my hand like I'm about to slap him and say, "Don't make me hurt you, Steven. 'Cuz I will."

He shuts his eyes. Tears start flowing out of his eyes in buckets. He's bawling. He starts wheezing and his shoulders move up and down like he's about to have an asthma attack. But I don't let up.

"Stop it!" I shout right into his face. "I know you're faking it. I know you only pretend to have asthma to get Mom and Dad to feel sorry for you. But it's not gonna work now. So just stop it!"

He's wheezing harder now. I can't stand the sight of him. He's so damn sickly and weak. I feel like taking the kid and throwing him off the fire escape.

The next thing I know, I slap him hard right across the face. It's the first time I've ever hit him.

Steven touches his cheek. Then, without a word, he goes over to the window and climbs through.

CHAPTER 35

STEVEN STANDS QUIETLY with his back against a wall, while I look around the living room, which smells like a fucking ashtray. I check all the piles of newspapers to make sure they're not hiding anything. Then I look in the closets in the hallway outside the bathroom. There's nothing there except old suits and boxes of old shoes. My heart's pounding so fast, it feels like I'm running a hundred miles per hour. If the super catches us, we're dead, which is why the first thing I did was unrig the window and open it. The first sign of the super, and we're out of there.

After I'm through with the living room, I check the bedroom. In the far corner, there's a picture of a woman in her 40s. Underneath the picture, there are a dozen candles. I don't know what it is about spics, but they always got a ton of candles.

Anyway, I'm not finding shit. No Atari. No comic books. No nothing. I'm so pissed I think about taking a dump right there on the super's bed. A big pile of shit for a big pile of shit. It's like a Fatty joke.

Then I hear it. It's faint at first, but there's no mistaking it. It's keys jiggling in a lock.

I rush back out to the living room window. All we have to do is climb back out, and it'll be another clean getaway.

But fucking Steven just stands there like he's paralyzed all of a sudden.

"Let's go," I say, thinking what a chickenshit the kid is and why he's gotta be so damn weird all the time.

But he just looks right at me and smiles this evil smile.

"What the fuck you doing? We gotta get outta here!"

He doesn't move. Then it hits me. The kid's not frozen 'cuz he's scared. He wants to get caught just to get back at me. That's how much he hates my guts. What a kid. What a stupid fucking kid.

CHAPTER 36

M OM GIVES ME one of those slaps that can snap your neck if you didn't see it coming. It doesn't matter to her that there are cops all around us. Not that the cops give a shit that a kid's getting slapped right in front of them.

They just stare at us for a while, then go back to what they were doing, shuffling papers and shoving donuts in their mouths.

But it ain't the slap that gets to me. It's the look on Mom's face that says I'm the biggest disappointment of her life and she regrets ever having me.

She then turns to Steven, who's crying buckets like the crybaby he fucking is.

"I'm sorry, Mom," the kid says, then buries his face in her stomach like he'd go back there if he could.

She rubs the back of his head and says, "It's okay, Steven. It's okay."

Some stupid cop comes over and says, "It looks like they got carried away playing detective. Your super, Mr. Da Silva, says he won't press any charges. But they'll still have to go before a judge. He'll decide what to do with them. But don't worry, whatever happens, we'll keep their record with us only until they turn 18. After that, their records will be sealed and it'll be like nothing ever happened."

Mom just nods, then goes with the cop to sign some forms. Steven sits back down. He's crying so hard there are snot bubbles in his nose. He doesn't even bother to wipe them away.

Another dumb cop comes over to me and says, "See what you're doing to your mother? Less than two percent of you people are into crime. You must be real proud of yourself."

I got eyes. Why the hell do I need him to remind me what I'm doing to my mother?

Fucking cops. They all think they know so fucking much. As

smart as they fucking think they are, I'll bet a thousand bucks not one of them could do the fucking Rubik's Cube.

I feel like taking his gun and putting a couple of bullets right through the guy's fat head. Then I'd blast my way out and catch a freight car to some other state and be on the run from the cops until I grow up and fight the gang boss there for control of the syndicate. Then I'll come back to Elmhurst in a limo covered with diamonds and hand out hundred-dollar bills to all the loonies in the Leben Home.

Anyway, when we finally get the hell out of there and go home, I half expect Mom to put my shit in a milk crate and kick me out like how Dr. Doom sent Nathaniel packing, but Mom doesn't do that. She doesn't even bother to hit me with the extension cord. Instead, she just leaves me alone like I wasn't even there. Who knows why grown-ups always think the silent treatment does anything? Fuck if I care if she talks to me or not. Fuck her and all her fancy ideas. Who the hell's she kidding? We're nobodies. What do I need to go to some fucking boarding school in Canada for? All they do is fucking speak French and play hockey. What the fuck do I need that for?

So I broke into the super's apartment. So what? The guy broke into mine, and no one seems to give a fuck about that.

So I go to my room and stare at the ceiling from my bed. The Fourth of July's still a day away, but fireworks are going off like crazy all over the place. Fucking Fatty and Africa are probably out there, too, lighting jumping jacks and laughing their asses off about how I got what was coming to me.

I try not to think about everything that's happened. My Atari's gone, and I'll never get it back. And there's not a damn thing I can do about it. That's just how things are. Not everything can be fixed, no matter how hard you try or how bad you want something. They might not tell you that at school, but that's the truth. I guess I always knew that, but a small part of me wanted to see if it really was true.

I don't know why, but I start thinking about how Mom and Dad would sometimes tease me when I was little by telling me how they found me under some bridge or bought me off some bum for a dozen empty bottles. Stuff like that used to get me all riled up back then. But now I'm older. So I know it ain't true. And even if it was, big fucking deal. Dad was an orphan, and he turned out all right, didn't he?

Dad comes home late as usual. I almost wish he'd beat the shit out of me, but he doesn't lay a hand on me. Instead, he just stands by the side of my bed for a long while without saying a word. Then he says, "When you go to the judge, Minho, make sure you look him in the eyes. What you did wasn't right. But it isn't like you killed anyone. Don't look down at your feet or beg. You just look him in the eye and let him know you're still strong."

Something about him saying that and not being even a little bit angry with me makes me feel so damn bad. And even though it ain't like I wanna grow up to be a gangster or a murderer or nothing like that, I can't help thinking how much it sucks to have parents, 'cuz you can't ever do nothing really bad without feeling all crummy about it. But I ain't sorry. And I don't care if the judge sends me and Steven to Spotfit. So there will be just black kids there. Big fucking deal. I've already been through Star Lake and I came out all right. Who the fuck knows? Maybe we'll even see a couple of kids from Star Lake there and we'll have ourselves a reunion.

For the rest of the night, I just lie there on my bed and try not to listen to Mom and Dad's shouting through the walls. It's the same shit they always argue about when they get mad about how she's not taking good care of me and Steven and how he's not strict enough and how there's never enough money. Considering how they were both teachers once, you'd figure they'd have something more original to argue about. It'd be better if they just chopped my head off.

From under my bunk, I hear Steven crying. The kid'll never learn. What good does fucking crying ever do?

Still, I lean over the bed and peer down at him. He's curled up on his side like some little baby. And I can't believe he and me are related.

All of a sudden, he looks up at me and says, "I hate you, Peter. I hate you so much. If Mom and Dad get divorced, I swear to God, I'll never forgive you!"

I don't know what it is about what he said. Maybe it's the fact that the kid strung sentences together or that he actually shouted something at me. But I suddenly feel like the worst older brother who ever lived, worse than even B.J.

CHAPTER 37

I DON'T FEEL like leaving the house, even though it's hot as hell 'cuz our apartment traps heat like an oven. So I spend the whole morning lying in bed and staring at the ceiling and thinking about all the shows on TV I can't see 'cuz we don't got a TV no more.

It ain't that I'm depressed or about to have a nervous breakdown or anything like that. I just don't feel like going outside and running into kids I know. By now, probably everyone's heard about what happened. And who knows what kind of shit Fatty's been saying about me?

But then I start thinking, why the hell should I sit around moping just 'cuz of what Fatty might have said? Who the fuck gives a shit what dickheads like that think or say?

That's the thing with getting into trouble or having something bad happen to you. It don't matter how bad or crummy something seems. The last thing you wanna do is get all down on yourself and start acting all depressed.

No matter what happens, you gotta make like everything's great and you're having a blast. It's like you can get your ass kicked, but as long as you spring back up and start running around with your arms up and screaming how you just kicked the living shit out of the other guy, it's like you might as well have won. That way, no one can point their fucking fingers at you and try to put you down or feel sorry for you. Fuck them. As long as you're having fun, there ain't nothing anyone can say. All they can do is look at you and feel jealous.

And that's exactly how I stroll back into the park, not with my head down but like I fucking own the place. And when Fatty and Africa come up to me, I tell 'em everything, about how the cops tried to beat a confession out of me but I wouldn't tell them shit 'cuz I ain't no snitch, and how I kicked one cop in the balls and spat in another's face.

And they're listening to me and loving every second of it, especially when I tell them how I took a dump in the middle of the super's living room. Fatty loves that part and has me tell it again.

And I know then that no matter if what I did was right or wrong, and no matter what happens in the future and who we grow up to be, they'll always remember me as the kid with balls of steel who broke into the super's apartment and fucking stood up to the cops.

While we're all cracking up, Africa taps my elbow and motions to the street.

We all look over and see Jin, who's got on the same hooded sweatshirt and looks like he's been sleeping down in the railroad tracks. Who knows? Maybe the kid's living there now, like Steven's cat.

He ducks through the hole in the fence and comes over to us without saying nothing.

"What's up, Jin?" says Fatty.

Jin just nods.

"Yo, you want us to jump your brother for you?"

Jin turns and stares at him.

"That way you won't have to worry about him beating you up no more, bro."

"He never hit me."

"What the fuck you talking about? He beat the crap out of you. He fucking burned you with a cigarette."

"He never hit me. And he never burned me with no cigarette. So take it back."

"Take what back?"

"He never hit me. You got no right to say he hit me. So take it back."

"I think you gotta go see a psychiatrist, bro. I think you're flipping out."

Jin lets out a scream and starts swinging at Fatty. It's almost like he's possessed or something. It takes Africa and me both to pull him off Fatty.

"Damn! What the fuck is your problem, bro?" says Fatty, trying to play it off like he ain't freaked out.

Jin starts laughing all hysterically, then starts walking back out to the street. I guess the kid's really losing it. Pretty soon, he'll be in the fucking Leben Home smoking butts he picks up off the street.

"What the fuck is his problem?" says Fatty, shaking his head.

"Just don't mess with him," I say.

"What's the big fucking deal? Everyone knows his brother's a thug. Shit, I wouldn't be surprised if it was B.J. who ripped you off."

He spits on the ground, then says, "Where the hell's your little brother, by the way? My mom told me he's gotta go to jail, too. Is it true?"

"He and me have to go see some judge. Probably the judge'll have us go see some shrink."

"Yo, all I'm gonna say is, if they ship your ass to Spotfit, just don't bend down to pick up the soap. I don't want you two coming back as faggots."

"Don't worry, Fatty. We're never gonna be like you."

"Good one, bro. All I'm gonna say is, that little kid surprised me, bro. I didn't think he had it in him. No offense, bro. But I just always thought he was gonna stay a runt all his life, you know. I didn't ever think he was gonna be no juvenile delinquent. Now he's got himself a fucking rap sheet."

I don't say nothing.

There's a flash of lightning, and a drop of rain falls on my nose. I look up. The sky's black for the first time in weeks.

Then there's thunder, and rain starts gushing down in thick sheets.

Fatty and Africa rush across the street and duck under the awning outside the bowling alley.

But I just stand there in the middle of the park with my head tilted back. I can feel each drop hitting my face. It's like I'm being pelted by a hundred tiny bullets.

"What the fuck you doing, bro? Get out of the fucking rain!" Fatty shouts.

I don't say nothing. I just stand there and let the rain fall on me. So much has happened in the last two days. And all for what? A fucking Atari. At least the old guy in the book did it for a fish.

I don't even care anymore. All I can think about is that I'll be 13 come December. And Steven will turn nine next June. I'll always be four years older than the kid, even if he hates my guts forever.

Also from AKASHIC BOOKS

BOY GENIUS by Yongsoo Park
232 pages, a trade paperback original, $14.95, ISBN: 1-888451-24-6
"*Boy Genius* is a modern-day *Candide* . . . Yongsoo Park's combination of popular culture, high ideals, comedy, and serious intent makes for a joyride of a read."
—*Education Digest*

"Superb writing!" —*Clamor Magazine*

SOME OF THE PARTS by T Cooper
A Barnes & Noble Discover Great New Writers selection (fall 2002)
A Quality Paperback Book Club selection (February 2003)
264 pages, a trade paperback original, $14.95, ISBN: 1-888451-36-X
"Sweet and sad and funny, with more mirrors of recognition than a carnival funhouse, *Some of the Parts* is a wholly original love story for our wholly original age."
—Justin Cronin, author of *Mary and O'Neil*,
2002 PEN/Hemingway Award–Winner

SOUTHLAND by Nina Revoyr
Nominated for an Edgar Award
348 pages, a trade paperback original, $15.95, ISBN: 1-888451-41-6
"*Southland* merges elements of literature and social history with the propulsive drive of a mystery, while evoking Southern California as a character, a key player in the tale. Such aesthetics have motivated other Southland writers, most notably Walter Mosely." —*Los Angeles Times*

"If Oprah still had her book club, this novel likely would be at the top of her list." —*Booklist*

BEULAH HILL by William Heffernan
288 pages, trade paperback, $13.95, ISBN: 1-888451-40-8

"The whispered revelations that come spilling out of *Beulah Hill* are like ghostly voices you sometimes hear in the attic—soft, sad and disturbingly urgent."—*New York Times Book Review*

"William Heffernan is one of the rare mystery writers who cares about soul."—Martin Cruz Smith

ADIOS MUCHACHOS by Daniel Chavarría
Winner of a 2001 Edgar Award
245 pages, a trade paperback original; $13.95, ISBN: 1-888451-16-5

"Daniel Chavarría has long been recognized as one of Latin America's finest writers. Now he again proves why with *Adios Muchachos*, a comic mystery peopled by a delightfully mad band of miscreants, all of them led by a woman you will not soon forget—Alicia, the loveliest bicycle whore in all Havana."
—Edgar Award-winning author William Heffernan

SPEAK NOW by Kaylie Jones
A new novel by the daughter of James Jones
249 pages, hardcover; $22.95, ISBN: 1-888451-53-X

Clara Sverdlow has been stalked by Niko Kamenski, her high-school lover, for almost twenty years. A recently sober alcoholic in her mid thirties, she has found happiness in a tenuous new marriage to Mark, another recovering alcoholic. Yet the past lurks over them like a great shadow, always encroaching on their happiness.

"A rich and splendid book." —Roger Rosenblatt

These books are available at local bookstores.
They can also be purchased with a credit card online through
www.akashicbooks.com. To order by mail send a check or money order to:

AKASHIC BOOKS
PO Box 1456, New York, NY 10009
www.akashicbooks.com   Akashic7©aol.com

Prices include shipping. Outside the US,
add $8 to each book ordered.

YONGSOO PARK is a novelist, filmmaker, and playwright. His debut novel, *Boy Genius,* was recognized as a Notable Title for the 2002 Kiriyama Prize and as a finalist for the 2003 Asian American Literary Awards. A former Van Lier Fellowship winner at the Asian American Writers' Workshop, Park wrote and directed the seminal Asian American independent feature film, *Free Country* (1996). A graduate of Swarthmore College, he lives in Harlem with his wife, So Jene Kim.